The
Skeleton
Man

A Novel
by Jay
Bennett

THE
SKELETON
MAN

Franklin Watts / 1986
New York / *London* / *Toronto* / *Sydney*

Library of Congress Cataloging in Publication Data

Bennett, Jay.
The skeleton man.

Summary: When his Uncle Ed commits suicide, after
giving him $30,000 for his eighteenth birthday, Ray
receives death threats and becomes involved in a
dangerous sequence of events.
[1. Mystery and detective stories] I. Title.
P3552.E5464S54 1986   813'.54   [Fic]   86-11202
ISBN 0-531-15031-3

For Manny,
Dear and
beloved friend

The
Skeleton
Man

Chapter

1

On January 2nd he had become eighteen. On January 3rd, his father's brother took him to the bank on Norwich Street and then they went downstairs to the vault room and there he, Raymond Bond, filled out a card and signed a paper and was given a key and a vault box. Then he and his uncle went into a narrow room and closed the frosted glass door behind them, turned on the overhead light, and then his uncle took thirty thousand dollars out of a clean white envelope.

He laid the money, thousand dollar bill by thousand dollar bill, into the oblong metal box, his long fingers reflecting the overhead light.

He closed the box.

"This is yours, Ray. For your college education. Remember. It's all yours."

Ray was silent. He was taller than his uncle and his shadow on the pale yellow wall was angular and dark.

"You're not to touch it until you need it for your—"

His uncle's low voice faded into the silence.

"My tuition. And expenses."

"Only that. Or wherever I am I'll come back to haunt you."

There was a grim smile on his uncle's lean face.

"I promise, Uncle Ed."

"Give me your hand on it."

His uncle's grip was like iron. And Ray knew he would never violate his word to the man.

"And nobody is to know of this. Nobody."

Ray nodded.

"Never. At any time. No matter what happens."

Ray nodded again.

"And you're never to ask where this money came from."

Ray looked at him.

"Is that clear to you?"

His uncle's voice was hard.

"Yes," Ray said.

"Good."

Then they left the narrow room, its light turned off, its walls now dark again. They gave the box back to the attendant and went up the marble staircase out of the bank and into the gray wintry day.

Flakes of snow fell about them.

They stood there on the hard pavement, two lone figures saying nothing to each other. A car passed slowly by.

"Thanks, Uncle Ed," Ray said.

His uncle suddenly turned away without a word or gesture and walked rapidly up the long block.

Ray stood there watching, the vault key in his pocket, until he saw the dim black figure turn the corner and disappear. And all that was left was the thin fall of the snow. Thin and chilling.

Then Ray turned and walked away, too.

That was January 3rd.

On January 4th, Edward Bond was found lying dead on the snowy sidewalk just outside his midtown hotel. He had jumped from the twelfth floor.

There was a suicide note. It was to Ray.

> *I've done all that I ever wanted. There's no purpose in going on. Remember your word.*
>
> *Goodbye,*
> *Uncle Ed*

The body was broken but the face was pale and composed, the eyes open and staring up at the night sky, a cold smile in them.

Chapter

2

There were only three people at the funeral: Ray, his mother, and a slender, brown-haired woman who stood in the back of the small chapel and left when the short, bleak services were over.

Edward Bond had died as he had lived—a lone, solitary man.

And all he left behind was an oblong vault box.

Later, Ray came to look upon that box as a coffin box, waiting for his own body.

But that was later.

Chapter

3

He sat on the porch and looked through the bare branches of the trees till he could see the distant sparkle of the water of the inlet. There were but a few stars in the black sky and just a touch of winter breeze. He sat there, huddled in his windbreaker, his hands in his side pockets, his cap tight on his head.

He heard his mother open the front door and come out onto the porch. But she stayed near the door and did not come close to him. He did not turn to her.

"It's cold out here."

He didn't answer.

"Why don't you come inside?"

He shook his head. "Just thinking."

"You can think inside."

He said nothing.

"He'll never come back. He's dead."

"I know that."

"In time you'll forget him."

"No," Ray said.

She drew her coat tighter to herself. The light from inside the warm house lay on her dark hair, making it glisten.

"I know that," she said. "I'm just talking words."

"You are."

"Words."

He turned and looked at her standing in the warm light.

You once were beautiful, he said to himself, when I was younger, still a kid.

And then he thought, Some men still think you're beautiful. Some men.

"He was a hard person to understand," she said.

"I think I knew him."

She shook her head and her voice was low and almost intense.

"Nobody knew him, really knew him. He was like your father."

"Forget it," Ray murmured.

But she went on.

"Two brothers. Closed-up people."

"Leave my father out of this," he said.

She flinched. "All right."

"Just leave him out."

"I said I'm sorry."

But his bitterness broke through.

"All my life I've been hearing your side. I'd like to find him one day and hear his side of the marriage."

"Ray, please, I—"

He rode over her. "He'd have a lot to say to me. Right out of his heart."

"Ray."

"And I'd listen. To every word. Every single one of them. Yes."

Now he saw the deep, fearful hurt in her eyes and he turned away without speaking another word. Turned away and gazed through the bare trees to the sparkling inlet and wished it were summer with the sun on the soft waters and he on a boat and away from everything. Just lying on the deck of the small white boat and Laurie at his side.

Laurie.

Just lying there silently with her, on her boat, looking up at the sun, watching it go down the sky hour by silent hour till it fell into darkness.

His mother's pensive voice broke through his thoughts.

"He left nothing. Not a penny."

"Yes," Ray said softly.

She didn't say anything for a while and then she spoke again.

"I was hoping there'd be something for you."

"Nothing."

"He knew how much you want to be a lawyer. How it costs money. Money we don't have."

The lane in front of them was dark and still.

"He knew it," Ray said.

"I heard you tell him once . . . what you wanted to do with your life . . . how hard you were studying. He asked you and you told him. Right here on this porch. I was sitting on the rocker there."

"I remember."

"You told him, Ray."

"He listened."

Her lips tightened into a fine line. She still had small, good features.

"He listened. Listened and did nothing."

Ray was silent.

"Lived there in that hotel in the city and left you nothing. Not a thin dime."

Ray's gray eyes became hard.

"You say that as if he had committed a crime by not leaving anything to me."

"I didn't mean it that way."

"It sounded that way to me."

"I was just stating a fact. That's all I did. That's all."

But he wouldn't let her go.

"It was in your voice."

"Cut it out. Please, Ray."

"I tell you it was in your voice. In your face. All there."

"Ray, stop it."

She shivered and pulled her coat tighter about her and as she did, he said to himself, Why am I fighting her? What's in me tonight? Why am I hurting her so? Why?

Last night I dreamed of him lying on the sidewalk. Maybe it's that.

He saw her lips quiver and he thought she would go back into the house and leave him sitting there on the wintry porch.

Slam the door, fling the coat on one of the old chairs and go into the small, shabby living room and turn on the television set and sit there watching with vacant eyes one of her night shows—watching while her mind and heart were outside on the porch with him.

But she didn't move from the spot, just stayed there, half in the light of the house and half in the darkness of the porch.

Didn't move and didn't talk.

I should let her alone, he said to himself. She's a lost, defenseless woman. Scared, so very scared of life.

He was about to speak to her, with tenderness, but she spoke first.

"I'm upset," she said in shaky voice. "Terribly upset over the way he died."

"I am, too," he said.

"But I didn't like him, Ray. That is the truth."

"I know that," he said.

His voice was gentle now.

"I tried to. But I just couldn't."

"That's how life works out sometimes, Mom. Nothing you can do about it. That's how the ball bounces, as they say."

"What did you see to like in him?"

Ray didn't answer.

"In all the years how many times did you actually see him?"

"Maybe ten," Ray said.

She nodded. "There. He kept to himself all the time."

"I guess so."

"Kept to himself. Except when he felt like coming out here to say hello to you. His only nephew."

Ray was silent.

"He had nobody else but you in this world. When you really get down to it. Just you, Ray."

Just me, Ray thought. Or were there others?

"Came out when he wanted to. Never once invited you to come in and see him. Isn't that so?"

Ray shrugged.

"That's how it was."

"That's how he was."

He turned away from her and looked through the bare trees. The sparkle was now gone from the inlet water. All was cold and dark.

"Who was that woman?"

"What woman?" Ray asked.

"The one who stood in the back of the chapel."

"Oh."

He had almost forgotten. Almost.

"Did he ever tell you about her?"

She was there, back in the shadows of his mind.

"No."

"He must've left whatever money he had to her. Wouldn't you think?"

"Maybe he did. Maybe he didn't."

"He must've lived with her."

"No."

"How do you know that?"

"Because he told me he always lived alone. And I believed him."

"He left it to her. Regardless."

And he wanted to say to her, Mom, he left his money to me. To his only nephew. But he remembered his word to Edward Bond and he was silent.

"Left you nothing. And yet I always felt that in his strange way he liked you. I always felt that."

"I think he liked me."

And then he said to himself, No, it was deeper than that. He loved me. I'm sure of that.

But then he said to himself, Who is sure of anything in this life?

"Did he ever tell you what he did for a living?"

Ray shook his head. "No. I never asked. And he never said."

"What do you think it was?"

"I've no idea."

"He was always good at figures. Very good."

"Yes. He once helped me with a math exam. A trig final. Helped me pass it with a high mark."

"When was that?"

"Oh. About two years ago."

A car went slowly down the lane and then turned into a driveway two houses away. The lights of the car went out and then a door opened and shut. The metallic sound came up to them, and then there was night silence again.

"He had come in," Ray said. "I was busy studying and he asked me if I needed any help and I told him I could use some. So we went up to my room and we worked on the math for about three hours. And then he had some coffee and went back to the city. Just coffee. Wouldn't eat anything. That's how he was."

"You never told me that."

"I guess I forgot."

"When was it?"

"During the week. Springtime. You were working late that evening."

"You never told me," she said again.

"No," he said.

There are some things you keep to yourself, he thought. I guess that was one of them.

I felt warm and close to him in those hours, those three very short hours. Felt closer to him than to the father I never got to know.

Come to think of it, I never had anybody. Not even her. Not even my own mother. Always a shadow between us.

She moved away from the door and came close to him.

"Years ago he was an accountant for a large firm. One day he quit and went out to the Coast for a long time. Then he came back and went to live at that hotel. Always stayed there."

"And that's where he died," Ray said.

"Yes."

She stood by his chair now. He could barely see her in the thick, enveloping darkness.

Then he heard her voice.

"So he helped you."

"Very much."

"I never knew it."

When she spoke again, her voice was gentle and searching.

"I was sitting on the porch with him one summer evening, we were waiting for you, and just before dark he started to talk a bit and then his face became very sad and he stopped speaking for a while. And then he said, 'Ellen, I know you wonder about me. I often wonder about myself. But there's no use in even going into it. I'm a skeleton man.' "

"What?"

She nodded and all he could see was a dim, wavering shape.

"That's what he said."

And the dim gleam of her eyes.

"A skeleton man," he murmured.

"Then he dropped it. Never explained what he meant by that."

"You didn't ask?"

"No."

"Why not?"

She didn't answer him.

"Why not?" he asked again.

It was a long time before she spoke.

"Maybe I didn't want to know the answer," she said.

"What do you mean?"

Again the pause.

"Mom."

"I don't know, Ray. I just don't know."

"You're keeping something from me."

"No."

"You are."

"Ray, I'm honest with you. I just don't know."

He didn't question her anymore.

After a while, she touched him softly on the shoulder and then he heard the sound of her going inside.

He sat there, not moving.

At ten o'clock the wind started to come up strong and he stirred himself and rose to his feet.

He stood there looking at the bare branches of the old trees, gray and vague against the night. Stood there motionless, his hands gripping the railing of the porch. His eyes upon the trembling branches.

Then he turned sharply from the cold railing and went into the house.

She had already gone to bed.

He turned the lights out and slowly went up the dark stairs to his room. He opened the door to a vast dark silence.

It took a long time before he fell asleep.

Chapter

4

A low rattling sound made him open his eyes and sit up in bed. A cold sweat was on his forehead. He stared across the moonlit room to the chair and there sitting in it was his uncle—just sitting there and gazing mournfully at Ray, his face lean and tight, dark shadows deep around the eyes.

"Ray."

He moved his long arm beseechingly toward Ray and the rattling started again.

Ray shuddered.

The arm was now still and the dry rattling slowly ended.

"I miss you, Ray," the figure said in a very low whisper.

"Why did you do it?" Ray whispered.

"Do what?"

"Why did you jump and kill yourself?"

The figure shook its head noiselessly.

"But I never did kill myself."

"Uncle Ed."

"I'm alive. You see me before you now."

"Why did you do it?" Ray asked again, desperately.

His voice rose and echoed against the shadowy walls.

"Why?"

"I miss you, Ray."

"Why, Uncle Ed?"

Ray got out of bed and began to walk across the cold bare floor to the figure sitting in the chair.

The figure shivered.

"Don't come near me, Ray. Don't or you'll end up like me. A skeleton man."

"Uncle Ed."

"Not another step."

The figure raised its two hands and held the bony palms up and out to Ray and the dry bitter rattling broke out again and grew louder and louder until Ray had to stop stockstill and frantically cover his ears.

"No more," he moaned. "I can't bear it anymore. I can't."

And as he said the last words, the sound stopped abruptly, and his eyes opened wide.

Very wide.

There was no one in the room.

No one on the chair.

Only silence and the cold moonlight.

"Uncle Ed," he whispered.

But no one sat on the shadowed chair.

He knew then that he had been dreaming. A mad, hopeless dream.

He slept no more that night.

Chapter

5

He walked out of the back door of the diner and onto the windy parking lot, his face white and tired against the night. He looked about him, his hands trembling slightly, and there was Laurie waiting for him in her car.

The small Toyota gleamed in the darkness.

He got in silently and sat down beside her.

He closed his eyes and sighed.

Then he opened them again and smiled at her. She ran her hand through his brown wavy hair.

"Tired, Ray? You look it."

He nodded.

"Was a busy day."

"You always say that."

"It's always a busy day in there."

He worked in the kitchen on weekends. His mother knew the owner and had gotten him the job.

Laurie smiled gently at him.

"Where do you want to go?"

He shrugged. "You name it. Anything just to get away from here."

"How about the Golden Nugget?"

"Atlantic City?"

"Just a half hour away."

"I know that, Laurie."

"Well?"

He hesitated.

"It's just that I—"

"Yes?"

He looked away from her clear, dark eyes and out to the blinking lights of the diner's sign. They went on and off. On and off. Incessantly. He hated them.

Hated the way the chef worked him without letup every hot steaming minute of the long day. Trying to get Ray to quit the job because he wanted it for his own son.

Ray wondered how much longer he could hold on.

Then he said to himself grimly, As long as I want to. Nobody's breaking me down. Nobody.

He turned back to Laurie and looked at her dark long hair and clean features and he felt better.

He listened to her soothing voice.

"I feel like playing the slots, Ray. An hour."

He smiled at her. "Ah, come on, Laurie. Grow up."

"Then we can go wherever you want, Ray."

He shrugged. "You have an I.D. card for the casino?"

"Uh-huh."

"Whose is it this time?"

"My sister's. And I have one for you if you want to use it."

He didn't say anything.

"Can I go?"

"Just to play the stupid slot machines?"

"I'll cut it down to a half hour. How's that?"

There was an eager, almost childish look in her eyes and it made her more appealing to him.

"Ray?"

He laughed softly.

"You sound like a compulsive gambler. So help me."

She reached out and touched his hair again.

"Cut it out. I just feel an urge to play a little. What's wrong in that? Everybody does it."

"They do."

"So?"

"They throw their hard-earned money away. It's wrong."

"But they do it."

"The odds are stacked against them. It's a rip-off."

"But people win. And it's fun."

He was silent.

"Well?"

"Okay," he sighed. "Let's get moving."

"Want to drive?"

He shook his head.

"I'm too beat. It's either I'm out of condition or I'm beginning to hate that job more than I ever did."

"You say that every time."

"I mean it every time."

"Well, what else is there?"

"Nothing," he said. "Just plain nothing."

He kept looking at the diner's sign. On and off —endlessly.

"Kent is a nice town to live in," he said in a weary tone. "But there are very few places to make a buck here. Especially when you need one."

"Like all small towns."

"I guess so."

"How's the roof? Been able to do anything with it?"

"No. We need a new one. Money. We'd do better to get out of that old house and into an apartment. But she likes houses. Makes peanuts with her job as secretary and yet likes houses. That's my mom. You want her you can keep her."

"You're really tired, aren't you?"

He looked at her and slowly smiled.

"Let's hit the road," he said gently.

"Sure."

She started the motor up and turned on the lights. Then before she drove the car out of the lot she turned to him and they kissed.

"It's good to see you, Laurie," he said.

"The same, Ray."

Then he leaned back in his seat and relaxed as she drove the small shining car onto the highway.

There was very little traffic at that hour. They rode along, not speaking a word to each other. Every now and then the lights of oncoming cars would rush onto them, light up the black night and then the lights would rush by them, and the darkness would sweep down onto them again, leaving them alone and isolated.

And Ray thinking of his uncle wandering about in an eternal night, ever lost.

"How's your father?" he asked.

"Fine. Sends his regards."

"I like him," Ray said. "He's easy to be with. I like that in a person."

And he thought again of his uncle. Was he easy to be with? Yes, there were times. And even then, underneath it all . . . something . . . something shadowy and wrong . . . off center . . . yes, that was it . . . you just couldn't put your finger on it.

He heard Laurie's voice come softly to him. "Am I easy to be with?"

"At times."

"Only at times?"

"Uh-huh."

She laughed and he sat back listening to her laughter and feeling good and warm.

"Dad still wants you to change to medicine," she said.

"Still at it?"

She nodded.

"Says you'll make a truly fine doctor. His words, Ray."

"So I'll give him competition?"

"Right."

Ray smiled and shook his head.

"He did what he wanted to do. I'll do what I want."

"Your own thing."

"That about says it, Laurie."

A car passed by them, flaring the night, and then they were in darkness again. The light from the dashboard made their faces glow.

"What made you pick law?"

He didn't answer for a while and she asked again.

He turned to her.

"I honestly don't know."

"Just happened that way?"

"I guess so."

"No particular time when you can pinpoint it? You got up one morning and then decided you wanted to be a lawyer? Nothing like that?"

"No, Laurie."

"Strange."

"Maybe it is."

And then he said to himself, Maybe I'm not telling her the truth. Maybe I'm not telling myself the truth. Maybe something happened way back . . . something in my childhood . . . somehow I seem to feel that way. At night when I'm in bed, just before drifting off . . . some memory seems to come shadowing in. . . .

"Ray?"

"What?"

"I thought you were sleeping. Your eyes were closed."

"Oh."

"If you want to sleep I won't bother you until we're there."

"I'll stay awake."

"Okay."

And then for a while they didn't speak to each other. He lounged back in the seat and lazily studied her clean profile.

"Like what you see?"

"Yes."

"What do you see?"

"A very pretty girl."

"Who's with a very handsome boy."

"Knock it off, Laurie."

She laughed and then slowed the car down for the last toll booth. They were now on the outskirts of Atlantic City.

She turned to him.

"You'll come into the casino with me?"

He shook his head silently.

"Just for luck, Ray?"

"I'll wait for you in the lobby or out on the boardwalk."

"I've got the I.D. for you."

"You told me that."

"Won't you come in just to stand by me?"

He didn't speak.

"You don't like to see me throw away my father's hard-earned money. Is that it, Ray?"

"You're beating a dead horse, Laurie," he said.

She paid the toll and drove on.

"Why?"

"Laurie, I've never once gambled on anything. Not even a dime."

"Why?"

He looked away from her and saw in the near distance the harsh, blazing lights of the new hotels lining the shore.

"I don't know. I don't know a lot of things about myself."

"I just gamble for the fun of it, Ray. Not really to win."

"That's what they all say, Laurie."

Her lips thinned.

"Stop being cynical. It doesn't become you."

"I'm not being cynical."

"You are."

He looked at her and then turned away and shrugged.

"I'm just telling it as I see it," he said.

"Then don't."

"You asked for it."

"I didn't."

They drove silently along, getting closer and closer to the row of casinos.

"Let's not get into a hassle, Ray," she said quietly.

Too quietly, he thought.

It was a bad sign.

"I'm not trying to."

"You're moving close to it."

"I'm not."

"Don't get my back up. You'll be sorry for it."

He looked at her set face and began to retreat.

"Okay, Laurie. Okay."

She shook her head and her hair swung and shimmered.

"I'm Scotch-Irish. That's a bad combination to mess around with."

"I'm not messing around with you."

"Good."

"Peace."

"Peace."

But her eyes were still flashing at him.

"Then you're definitely not coming in with me."

"Right."

"Wish me luck."

"You've got it," he said gently.

They stopped at an intersection and now the

lights of the casinos were all about them, hemming them in.

A red reflection from one of the huge garish signs fell directly across the car.

Like a sharp, bloody wound.

Ray felt a chill settle over him.

A chill of fear.

Chapter

6

He walked along the boardwalk till he was out of the lights and the shine of the hotels and then he strolled over to the iron railing and stood there looking out to the sea. The night was not too cold but the wind was up, whipping the sand and the water. With an anger.

He stood there, hunched over the railing, his eyes going past the white-topped waves and trying to pierce through the dark horizon. He thought he could see the glimmering lights of a large passenger ship, way, way out, and it was then that he felt someone come up to the railing and stand near him.

He tensed and he didn't know why.

"You have nine dollars?"

Ray turned. "No," he said.

The man was lean and well-dressed but he had a haunted look in his eyes.

"They stripped me clean."

Don't they always? Ray thought.

"Clean to the bones."

"I'm sorry."

"This sounds crazy, but I need the nine for parking."

It always sounds crazy with these fellows, Ray thought grimly.

"I got my car in a lot. They won't give me the car without my paying the fee. I come up short nine dollars."

"I don't have it."

"You sure? I'll mail you back fifty."

"Sorry."

Ray swung away from him and stared out at the white foam of the breakers. He waited for the man to drift on. But the black-coated figure stayed there, at his side. Like a black shadow.

"Nine dollars. You must have nine you can spare. I'd give you my watch but they stripped me even of that. I pawned it this afternoon. The money's gone. Hit a lucky streak and then along comes this downer and I'm clean."

"You're wasting your time with me," Ray said.

"You won't lend me the money?"

His haunted eyes held Ray.

"Nobody else did, did they?"

"No."

"So why come to me?"

Yet the eyes of the man would give him no peace.

"You won't lend it to me?"

"No."

"Why not?"

Ray didn't answer.

"Because you don't have it?"

"I have it," Ray said.

"But still you won't lend me the money?"

"Still."

"It's only nine dollars."

"I said, no."

The man turned away silently and left him. Ray turned back to the sea and searched for the lights of the boat but they were gone.

Only empty darkness remained. Darkness and the lost, haunted eyes of the man.

And then he heard the pleading voice again.

"Here. I'll leave this for the nine dollars."

He held in his gloved hand a softly shining disc.

"What is it?"

"A medal."

"I don't want it," Ray said.

"I'm a vet. It's the Congressional Medal of Honor."

Ray looked up from the medal and into the eyes of the man. And for an instant, a flashing instant, he thought he could see the sad, sad eyes of his dead uncle.

As he saw them in the dream.

"That's all I have left. I'm clean. Bone clean."

Ray didn't speak. All he could hear was the bleak sound of the wind over the waves. And he suddenly felt cold, cold to his very soul.

"It's the real thing. I almost died for it." The man's voice seemed to come to him from a distance. "The real thing."

"Yes," Ray said in a low voice.

"Spent a year in an army hospital. It's the real thing."

The medal glinted in the black-gloved hand.

"Take it and give me nine. Just the nine. I've got to get out of this hard town and go home. I want to go home. Home."

His voice broke.

Ray felt ashamed, as if the man had stripped himself naked before him.

"I don't want the medal," he said and took his wallet out of his inside jacket pocket.

He silently gave the man a ten dollar bill.

"I only wanted nine."

Ray shook his head.

"Take it," he said.

"Thanks."

The man set the medal into Ray's hand and closed his fingers over it.

"Keep it," he said. "Until I send the fifty I promised you."

"I don't want it."

"It's yours till then."

"I don't want the medal and I don't want the fifty."

"Take good care of it."

"I said I don't want it."

But the man wasn't listening to him anymore. He had turned his head away from Ray and was staring into the wind-lashed sea.

His eyes filled with a desperate longing.

"Home," he whispered to himself. "I'm finally going home."

He turned and looked fully at Ray, as if seeing him for the first time. Then he swung abruptly away and disappeared into the darkness.

Ray stood there bewildered and then he stirred himself.

"Wait," he called out and began to run after the man. "Wait. You didn't give me your . . . You don't know where I live. . . . You—"

But the wind blew away his words.

"Wait!"

He never found the man. He had lost him down one of the dark sidewalks that led off the boardwalk. Lost him forever.

"He's gone," Ray muttered. "Gone."

He leaned despondently against the cold brick wall of an old and abandoned hotel, a building that was soon to be torn down to make way for another neon-lighted hotel.

Another casino that would strip other men and women to their very bones, he thought bitterly.

Making them cry desperately to go home.

Home.

Ray walked slowly back onto the windswept boardwalk.

He paused under the bleak light of a street lamp and looked down at the medal glowing in his hand. And he thought of the lost man and he wanted to weep.

Chapter

7

When Laurie came out of the casino her face was flushed with success.

"You brought me luck, Ray."

"Did I?"

"I won fifty dollars."

"That's good."

"Where do you want to go? We'll spend the fifty."

"Home," he said.

"What?"

"That's what I said. Home, Laurie."

She looked at him and his face was white and drawn.

"All right," she murmured.

They drove back in silence, a long distance. Then she turned to him.

"What happened, Ray?"

"Nothing."

"Won't you tell me?"

He shook his head.

"Come on, Ray."

"Just let it alone, Laurie."

"Anything I did?"

He shook his head again.

"Anything I said?"

"No."

"We made peace."

"We did," he said.

She leaned forward to him.

"Say it again."

"Peace, Laurie."

"Peace, Ray."

She waited a while and then she spoke again in a soft voice.

"So?"

"Just let it rest."

"Okay."

She stopped for a toll booth and she reached over and touched his hair tenderly. He felt a warm glow start in him.

"Just let me be for a while," he said.

"Okay. I won't push it."

Then later on she got him to smile again and they had a good time together. But underneath it all, the darkness remained with him.

The darkness of the stripped, lost man.

Chapter

8

He took the oblong metal box and went into the room with the overhead light and closed the frosted glass door. Then he opened the box and looked at the money that was in it. The thirty thousand dollars. He stood gazing at the crisp bills. Then he put his hand into his pocket and took out the medal.

It glinted coldly under the overhead light.

He stood there looking at the medal.

He could almost hear the man's haunting voice break through the stillness.

"It's the real thing. The real thing."

"Yes," Ray murmured. "It is."

Now he could see the deep, sad eyes. Coming out of the shadowy corner of the room. Ray's hand closed over the medal.

"I died for it," he heard the voice whisper into his ear.

Ray shook his head. "Almost," he said.

"No," the voice whispered. "I died. I'm still lying on that bloody battlefield. I never left it."

"No."

"I'm lying there. You met a ghost," the voice whispered.

Ray trembled and looked about him to see if anyone else was in the narrow room with him.

But he was alone. Alone under the overhead light.

"I died for it," he heard the voice whisper again. "Only to throw it away on a crap table in a noisy casino."

"You didn't die," Ray said desperately. "You didn't throw it away. I'll take care of the medal for you. I promise you that."

"Will you?" The voice laughed, a harsh, cynical laugh.

"Yes. I promised you."

The voice laughed again. "Wait. Wait till you find out what life is about. Wait till you meet all the liars and thieves in this world. Wait till you become a liar yourself."

"I'll never be that."

The voice went on relentlessly.

"Till you become a thief."

"Never."

"A murderer."

"What?"

"Yes. Till murder comes into your heart."

"No. Not that."

"It does to everyone, Ray. It will to you."

"Never, I tell you."

"Wait. Just wait."

The voice faded away.

And there was silence.

Only silence.

Ray stood there gazing at the shadowy corner and then he stirred himself and breathed out a low sigh.

He opened his hand and gently laid the medal upon the green bills and then slowly closed the narrow metal box.

Then he turned out the light and shut the door.

He handed the box to the silent attendant and went up the marble staircase and out into the open winter air.

A woman was standing on the opposite corner, gazing at him. She was slender and she had brown hair.

He wanted to cross the street to talk to her. But she turned swiftly and went away into the darkening afternoon.

Chapter

9

He was sitting in his room, waiting for his mother to come home for the dinner he had prepared for them, when he heard the phone ring downstairs.

He put down the textbook he was reading and then went down the silent staircase and into the hallway and picked up the phone.

The long shadows of evening were just coming into the house. He had not as yet turned on the lights.

"Hello?"

"Raymond Bond?"

It was a voice he did not know.

"Yes."

The man's voice was soft, pleasant and precise.

"We want to talk to you."

Almost like that of Mr. Wallace, his physics teacher. A teacher he liked very much. But this voice chilled him.

"We?"

"That's right. Your uncle was a friend of ours."

"And?"

"He left some unfinished business behind him."

"I don't follow you."

"You will after we talk."

Ray just stood there and didn't speak.

Out on the porch the rocker moved up and back, with a steady easy rhythm.

Up and back.

But nobody sat on it.

Only the soft wind.

"How about the park where you sit with your girl friend after school?"

"What?"

"But don't bring her along. We want to talk to you alone. Be sure to come alone. Be very sure."

"Who are you?"

"How about three o'clock tomorrow, Ray?"

"Who?"

But there was no answer.

Only a click.

Chapter

10

"Mom."

She looked up from her dinner.

"My father. Is he dead?"

"What?"

"Tell me. Is he dead or alive?"

"I don't know."

"When was the last time you heard from him?"

"Years ago."

He looked across the table at her. "How old was I when I last saw him?"

"Two. Just two years old."

"You're divorced?"

"Yes."

"You sometimes made me feel he was alive. Very much alive."

"I did."

"You loved him?"

"Once."

"And now you hate him."

"Yes."

He was silent and she just sat there looking across the table at him. Her spoon gleamed on the white tablecloth. She always liked to have dinner on a white tablecloth.

"Why are you asking me these questions?"

He noticed a stain on the tablecloth where she had dropped her spoon. A yellowing stain. He didn't answer her. For he didn't know himself. The questions had come from deep within him. Suddenly. Without warning.

"Why, Ray?"

"I don't know," he said. "I just don't know."

"There must be a reason."

"Just got curious. That's all."

"Why?"

"Let me alone, Mom," he said softly.

"No. You must tell me."

He could see her hands beginning to tremble.

"It's nothing."

"Please, Ray."

And now the look of fear had crept into her eyes.

"Mom," he said soothingly. "The questions have been in me for years. And now they've come out."

"Why now?"

"I don't know. I just don't know."

"But—"

"From out of nowhere," he cut in. "Just from out of nowhere."

She shook her head.

"Something's wrong. Something's happened."

"Nothing, I tell you."

"Ray."

"Nothing. Just got curious."

He got up from the table and went outside onto the porch and stood there looking out to the gray trees. Through their leafless branches he could see the pale waters of the inlet.

He heard his mother come out to him.

"He's dead," she said.

Ray did not turn.

"He died in jail."

"Why? What did he do?"

"He took money from the bank. He worked there. And stole money."

"Why?"

He had to ask her again.

"He was a gambler," she said.

"No."

"He gambled everything away. Everything. Till there was nothing left. Not even his pride."

They looked at each other and then he saw the tears starting in her eyes and he turned away from her.

He couldn't bear seeing her agony.

He didn't even hear her go back into the house.

Chapter

11

It rained late that night, a cold winter rain, and the slash of the rain against the windows and its steady beat on the roof above woke him up.

All else about him was quiet except for the cold incessant sound of the rain. All but that.

He lay in bed, his eyes half-closed, and he thought of the man who had phoned him. Through the sound of the rain he heard again the voice. Low and whispering. A soft rhythm.

Tomorrow, Ray.

Tomorrow.

At three.

Come alone.

Be sure to come alone.

Be very sure.

He lay there listening to the voice slowly fade away into the warm darkness.

His eyes almost closed again.

And then he thought, If the rain keeps up through the day, will the man be sitting on the bench in the park? Sitting under a large, black umbrella waiting for me?

And then somehow, into Ray's sleepy consciousness, the figure of another man drifted in. Dark but clearly defined.

That must be my father, Ray thought, I'm sure it is.

Even though I've never really seen him, I'm sure it is.

His eyes are like my Uncle Ed's.

His face lean and quiet.

So very quiet.

So motionless.

Like a death mask.

Then he saw the two sitting there on the same bench, side by side, under their black umbrellas . . . the unknown man and his unknown father . . . waiting for him . . . ever waiting for him.

And then his eyes closed over the hazy vision and he was asleep.

12

"You're not talking much, Ray."

"Didn't realize it, Laurie."

"Something on your mind?"

He shook his head silently.

"Something heavy?"

"Everything's okay, Laurie," he said.

It was getting close to three o'clock. Very close.

"You sure?"

"Uh-huh."

They walked along, side by side, and when they came to the corner he stopped first.

"Laurie."

She stopped and looked up at him. "Yes?"

"I can't sit with you today."

"Oh?"

Her eyes were probing into him.

"I've got to take care of something."

"I guess you do."

"Something for my mother."

He didn't feel comfortable with the lie and he wondered if it showed. It was not easy to fool Laurie. Never was.

"And you have to do it alone?"

He nodded. "Yes."

And as he said that, he wondered to himself, Why is it that I always do things by myself?

When the chips are down, really down . . . one is always alone. And then he thought, but the man wants me to be alone. He made that very clear.

Ray heard Laurie's voice. "Then that's how it is."

"Yes."

"I'll see you tomorrow?"

"Sure thing."

"We'll walk to school together?"

"We always do."

"Tomorrow?"

"Sure, Laurie. I'll wait on the porch for you," he said.

"Eight?"

"On the head."

She leaned forward and kissed him lightly on the cheek.

"So long, Ray."

"So long, Laurie."

He thought she would go, but she still stayed at

his side. The light changed to green for her but still she did not move.

"It's a nice day."

"Yes. It is, Laurie."

"Think it will snow again soon?"

"It has to."

"Yes," she echoed dully. "It has to."

"You always liked snow."

But she didn't seem to be listening to him anymore.

"Peace," she suddenly said, in a low and trembling voice.

And he wondered why she said that.

And why her voice trembled.

"Peace, Laurie," he murmured

They waited silently for the light to change to green again. Then he stood there watching her cross the street safely and go down the next block, slowly and surely disappearing from him. And as he stood there, his body rigid, his eyes ever on her, he wished with all his heart that he could go along with her.

But he knew that he couldn't.

The three o'clock appointment was waiting for him.

Chapter

13

When he came to the bench a man was sitting there, gazing off toward the playing field. He was smoking a pipe.

"Raymond Bond?"

Ray nodded silently.

"Sit down."

"All right."

"I'm Albert Dawson."

Ray sat there waiting for the man to speak again. But Dawson puffed quietly on his pipe and kept his eyes fastened on a spirited game of touch football. The dark figures of the players were small in the distance and their voices drifted faintly through the air.

The day was bright and cold.

"You do any sports?"

The man had not yet turned to him.

"Some football."

"For the school team?"

"I did it for a while. But then I gave it up."

"Not good enough?"

"No. It wasn't that."

"What was it?"

Ray shrugged. "I guess it was taking time from my studies. Too much time."

The man now turned and looked at him speculatively. "I see."

He had iron-gray hair and quiet blue eyes. He was dressed in a form-fitting blue overcoat. A light tan felt hat.

He was tall, just over six feet. Tall and slender. He had a gray chin beard. Neatly trimmed.

His gloves were black.

"You're planning to be?"

The voice was soft and pleasant, the articulation precise.

Just like Mr. Wallace, Ray thought. Just like him. And yet so deadly different. I can feel it in my bones. Yes.

"A lawyer," Ray said.

"I see. I was a lawyer once."

"And?"

"Quite a successful one. But I gave it up. For better things."

What better things? Ray thought.

Dawson was silent.

Ray waited.

Out on the playing field a touchdown was scored and Dawson smiled.

It was a pleasant smile. The lines about the blue eyes crinkled and the finely-shaped lips parted ever so slightly.

You're a very attractive man, Ray thought. Attractive and deadly. One can feel it just sitting next to you.

"That was a fine catch, wasn't it, Ray?"

"I wasn't watching," Ray said.

"Oh. I thought you were."

"I wasn't."

"Your mind on other things?"

"Yes."

Dawson smiled.

"Of course it is. Thoughtless of me."

"You wanted to talk to me about my uncle," Ray said.

Dawson nodded. "I do."

"So let's do it."

"But first I want to get to know you better."

"Why?"

The man held up his gloved hand gently. The blue eyes hardened just a bit. But they were still pleasant.

"Let's do it my way."

Ray was silent.

"What position did you play?"

"Wide receiver."

The cool blue eyes studied him again. "You're rangy. Are you fast?"

"I guess so."

"How fast do you do the hundred?"

"Ten four."

"That's fast."

"I guess so."

"How are your hands?"

"My hands?"

"For catching a pass."

"Oh."

"Well?"

"Pretty good."

Dawson smiled. "Score a few touchdowns?"

"Yes."

The man's setting me up for something, Ray thought to himself. I've had that happen to me before. On the football field. They fake you out.

"You must have been a superb player."

"I was all right," Ray said.

"You're modest. You were a credit to your team. I'm sure of that."

"Maybe."

"It was a great sacrifice for you to give it all up. Wasn't it?"

"Sort of."

"Your career means everything to you, doesn't it?"

"Yes."

Dawson patted him softly on the shoulder. "You're not one of these strung-out athletes, are you? You're not a jock, either. You have texture and fiber."

He patted Ray again. "It's a pleasure to meet you, Ray. You don't mind my calling you Ray, do you? If you do, please tell me."

"I don't mind."

"Excellent. We're going to get along together. I'm sure of that."

Are we? Ray thought, looking at the clean, sharp profile of the man. You're not like Mr. Wallace at all. You put a chill in me.

Dawson had paused to relight his pipe. Now he turned back to Ray.

"What do you know about your uncle?"

"Know?"

Ray felt himself tense up, in every little nerve.

"His way of life. How he made his living. His friends. His interests."

Ray didn't answer.

"Well?"

"Nothing much."

"You really mean nothing. You knew absolutely nothing about him."

"I guess you're right."

Dawson nodded.

"I thought so. Nobody knew anything about him. Except for a very few people. That's the way he wanted it. And that's the way he kept it. He was a man who went through life deceiving everybody. Nobody knew what he did. He was a gambler, Ray."

He said the last words so quietly and so smoothly that for a moment Ray did not grasp their meaning.

"That's all he was."

"What?"

Ray's face had whitened.

"Yes, my boy. Edward Bond was a gambler. A lifetime gambler. Nothing more nor less."

"I don't believe you," Ray said.

Yet deep within he did believe.

Two brothers, he thought bitterly to himself, two brothers with the same disease.

"I didn't expect you to believe me," Dawson said.

Then they both were silent.

He had me set up, Ray said fiercely to himself. Set me up and then faked me out. Completely.

I'm down on my back on the grass. Everything is dark and twisted. My feelings all tangled up.

He just smashed something for me. What my mother had told me about my father somehow didn't hit me as much as this does. My father was never part of my life. Never.

Uncle Ed was all I had, the little I ever saw him. So little. But he was all I had. And now he's gone, too.

Out on the playing field the game broke up. The dark figures came close to each other, in clusters, and then separated. Each went his own way, and soon the field was empty. Empty and flat, under the winter sky.

"Did you know him?" Ray asked tonelessly.

"Yes. I knew him. Knew him enough to lend him some sums of money over the years. All of which he eventually paid back. With interest."

"It's always with interest. Isn't it?" Ray said in a harsh voice.

"Yes, my boy. Always."

"Big interest."

"Big. No doubt about that. Otherwise how could I exist?"

"That's true," Ray said coldly. "How could you?"

"You understand, don't you?"

"Yes."

"I don't impress you as being a saint, do I? One who gives money to people out of the great and good generosity of his heart. Do I, Ray?"

"You don't."

"I have impressed some gullible people in my day. But not you. That's quite evident, my boy."

Ray turned away from the gentle, almost mocking smile and looked out at the desolate field.

"You say he always paid you back."

"I said that."

"So why do you want to see me?"

"He paid me back. Except for the—"

Dawson deliberately paused and puffed on his

pipe and said nothing more. His blue eyes quietly appraised Ray.

"Except?"

And Ray already knew the answer.

He trembled before the man spoke again.

"Except for the last loan."

"The last one?"

"Just before he died. It was for the amount of thirty thousand dollars."

So that's it.

That's where the money came from.

"He owed me thirty thousand dollars. And then he jumped from a window."

Ray clenched his hands and then slowly opened them again. "He jumped."

"And left the debt behind him."

They were silent.

"You say he was a gambler," Ray said quietly. "Then he must have gambled the money away."

Dawson shook his head.

"He didn't."

"How do you know that?"

"We know."

"We?"

"I am not alone, my boy. I have others with me."

"Then what did he do with the money?"

Dawson smiled his pleasant smile, yet his eyes were cold and piercing.

"That is why we're sitting here on this chilly

afternoon. Sitting, trying to find out what he did with the money. Perhaps you can tell me, Ray."

"I?"

"You were his only near relative. His nephew."

"So?"

"He didn't give it to you?"

"Why to me?"

"You're not answering my question."

"He never gave me a dime. He may have gambled thousands of dollars away but he was tight with me and my mother. We never got anything from him. Nothing, I tell you, nothing."

"You're a man of truth, Ray," Dawson said gently. "I'm convinced of that."

"I'm telling you the truth."

Dawson shook his head.

"Listen to me. I rarely make mistakes in judging character. If I make a bad one, a truly bad one, then I am dead. That's the nature of my existence. You understand that, don't you?"

Ray was silent.

"I live in a violent world. It can be very serene for quite a time and then suddenly it gets very violent. People die."

Ray still didn't speak.

"Well? The money."

"He didn't give it to me."

Dawson shook his head again.

"You were seen going down into the bank vault."

Ray's hands quivered.

"What do you keep there?"

"Just some things."

"What things?"

"My father's dead."

"So?"

"I keep his medal there."

"Oh?"

"The Congressional Medal of Honor."

"Your father won it?"

Ray nodded.

"He was killed in the war."

"And he left it behind for you?"

"Yes."

"You should be proud of him, Ray."

"I am."

"He was your uncle's brother?"

"Yes."

"Your uncle never said a word about him. Not a solitary word."

"They never had much to do with each other."

"What else is in that box?"

"The medal is very precious to me," Ray said.

"I am aware of that."

"I didn't want to lose it. So I put it in the box."

"Understandable. What else?"

"In the box?"

"In the box, Ray."

"Some pictures of him. In his army uniform."

"And?"

"His gold watch that he left me."

"That is all?"

"All. You asked for the truth and I gave it to you," Ray said.

"You did."

"There's nothing else in the box. Nothing."

"Nothing," Dawson softly echoed.

He gently hit the bowl of his pipe against the edge of the wooden bench and then he carefully put the pipe away in his coat pocket.

"Ray, that money is ours. We want it back."

"I have no money."

"We always get it back."

"I don't have it."

"Always."

"But I tell you that I don't—"

The black-gloved hand was raised and Ray abruptly stopped speaking.

"We'll talk again."

"There's no reason to."

"Let me be the judge of that."

Dawson rose to his full height and looked down at Ray.

"How old are you?"

"Eighteen."

"That's too young an age to die. Especially with such a brilliant career in law ahead of you. Think of that, my boy."

Then he smiled, a bleak smile, and walked away.

Chapter

14

He dreamed that night that his father and his uncle were playing cards down in the kitchen. They sat at the table, just the two of them, and it was night, and they were alone in the entire house. Just the two of them.

They played silently. Stud poker.

His father shuffled the cards and then began dealing out the new hands. "I'm on a hot streak."

"You sure are."

"I've won enough money. This is the last hand and we quit."

"Okay."

"What are the stakes for this one?"

"I told you when we started."

"I forgot."

Their faces had become somber. Their eyes dull and gleaming. Their voices flat and hollow.

"We're playing for Ray's life."

"Yes. I remember now."

"You win and Ray lives."

"Correct."

"I win and he dies," his uncle said.

"He dies."

Ray stood in the doorway of the kitchen and watched them with a cold dread. His shadow was large upon the kitchen floor.

They played without a word passing between them and then his father spread out his hand and it was three kings and two queens.

A full house.

Ray felt a surge of joy go through him.

"I win," his father said. "Ray lives. You can't beat this one."

"I can't?" There was a derisive smile on his uncle's lips.

"What've you got?"

"Take a look."

His uncle slowly spread out his cards on the kitchen table. They gleamed in the cold light. A royal flush.

"Nothing beats a royal flush," his father whispered.

"Nothing."

"You ever get one in all the days and years that you've played cards?"

His uncle shook his head. "Never."

"Neither did I."

His father looked again at the spread cards. "I never expected it to happen this way."

"It happened."

"You can't beat chance."

"No. You can't."

"We're fools. Both of us," his father said in a mournful hollow voice. "All our lives we tried to beat chance. And we lost."

"In the end you lose. You have to lose."

"Yes."

They both were silent, looking coldly at the spread cards.

"Ray dies," his uncle said, in a harsh and final voice.

"He dies."

And it was then that Ray cried out and woke up.

"No," he whispered to himself. "No."

He got out of the moonlit bed and went to his window and looked out at the slowly waning night.

A long dreary time.

Two gamblers, he said bitterly to himself.

They'd gamble away anything.

Even one's life.

Chapter

15

The two walked along side by side, saying little to each other. The morning lay quiet about them. When they came onto the school grounds, he stopped and turned to her, his face white and somber.

"Laurie."

"Yes?"

They stood under a large bare oak tree, away from all the others. Alone in their private world.

"Laurie," he said in a low voice. "I'm in trouble."

"What do you mean?"

He shook his head.

"Don't ask me. Just listen."

"But—"

"Listen. Please."

She looked up at him and slowly nodded. Her eyes ever on his face.

"All right," she murmured.

"I can't tell you what the trouble is. You're never to ask me."

"Ray, I—"

"Never."

She was about to speak but he raised his hand gently and touched her cheek and then softly stroked it. A sad, poignant look in his eyes.

"That's the way it has to be."

"I don't understand."

"Don't try."

"It's not fair. I want to help you."

"There is no help," he said.

"I still want to know."

He shook his head.

"You say it's not fair. When was life fair, Laurie? You tell me. It's just thrown me a mean curve. From out of nowhere. And that's how it is."

He stopped speaking and turned away from her.

"Ray." Her voice was soft and pleading.

"Laurie, don't," he said. "Just knowing that you're there is enough for me. That's all I really need. It'll help me through."

"Whatever it is, you can't do it alone."

"I have to. You don't understand."

"Then tell me, and I will."

"No."

"It's not fair to me."

"Let it alone."

"No. You know how I feel about you."

He didn't speak.

"Whatever happens to you, happens to me."

"I say let it alone. Don't make me sorry I opened up to you."

Her eyes flashed. "You didn't open up at all."

"I did."

"No."

She stood there in the gentle gleam of the morning light, looking at him, her face pale, so very pale.

And he said to himself, I shouldn't have started this with her. It was wrong. A bad move.

I should've kept my mouth shut.

She's being hurt, and that's the last thing I wanted to do to her.

To Laurie of all people.

Laurie.

But I had to turn to somebody. I had to.

"Ray."

He didn't answer her.

"Ray," she said again.

He slowly turned to her.

"You're making a bad mistake. I know that you are," she said.

"Then I'm making it. But that's how it has to be."

"You won't tell me?"

"No."

"Why?"

"We're talking in circles, Laurie."

She sighed. "I guess we are."

She was silent.

He reached out and touched her hair gently. "It won't do you any good to know anything more, Laurie," he said.

"I want to know. Whether it does me good or not."

"I'm trying to protect you. Can't you see that?"

She shook her head away from his hand.

"Protect me from what?"

"Forget it," he said.

"No. I won't."

"I've talked too much."

"You've got to tell me, Ray."

He shook his head grimly. "Stay out of it, Laurie. Just stay out of it."

And then he turned away from her and walked to the school building and went inside, not once turning back to look at her still standing under the bare branches of the oak tree. Not once.

I'm all alone now, he said to himself.

Alone.

Chapter

16

He picked up the phone, expecting to hear Dawson's voice.

"Hello?" he said.

But it was the voice of a woman.

"Ray Bond?"

"Yes?"

A voice he did not know.

"We've never met. But I was a friend of your uncle."

His hand tightened its grip on the black receiver.

"My uncle?"

"Yes. A good friend."

And he thought of the woman with the brown hair. The slender woman who stood in the back of the chapel and who saw him come out of the bank one afternoon.

"I'd like to see you."

"What about?"

"I'd rather not discuss it on the phone."

Ray was silent.

"It's to your advantage to see me."

"How do I know that?"

There was the slightest of pauses and then he heard her voice again. "Because I know of your problem with Dawson."

"What?"

"I want to help you."

He stood there thinking.

"But we've got to be careful. Very careful."

"Where do you want to see me?"

"There's a hotel in Louisville."

Louisville was the next town away.

"The Macklin," he said.

That was the only decent hotel there. On Somers Street. The other two hotels were small run-down places, on dreary side streets.

"Yes," she said. "The Macklin. I'm there now."

"Who shall I ask for?"

"Alice Cobb."

"Cobb?"

"Yes."

He searched back in memory. His uncle had never mentioned the name. And then he said to himself, He never mentioned any names of people

he knew, never to me. Dawson was right. I know
nothing about my uncle. But I'm getting an education now, a crash course on the strange life and ways
of Edward Bond. My benefactor. Now dead from
suicide.

A bitter smile had come to Ray's lips.

"When do you want to see me?"

"Could you make it five thirty this afternoon?"

"Five thirty?"

"I know it's short notice."

He thought and then he answered.

"All right."

"My room number is 418. I'll be waiting here
for you."

"I'll try to be there."

"You must." The voice had become urgent.

"I'll be there," he said.

"Till then, Ray."

And he thought she was going to hang up, but
she went on.

"Are you coming by car?"

"I don't have one."

"Is there a bus?"

"Yes."

"When you take it, make sure you're not
followed."

He became taut, silent and taut.

"Be very sure."

"Why?"

But she didn't answer him.

"If you feel anybody is following you, don't come to the hotel. Walk around the town as if you're shopping and then take the next bus back."

Ray didn't say anything.

"Are you there?"

"Yes."

"I'll get in touch with you again if that happens. Remember don't come near the hotel if you're followed. You'll be putting your life in great danger."

He stood there looking at the wall and he noticed a slight tear in the new blue wallpaper and he said to himself, I'll have to repaper that spot for Mom, lucky I have a roll left down in the cellar, wonder why Mom never told me about the tear, she's always so finicky about everything in the house, so finicky, and then he heard his voice, as if coming from another person.

"I won't come if I'm followed."

"Goodbye, Ray."

"Goodbye."

He slowly put down the phone, and as he did, it almost slipped from his grasp.

His hands were clammy and his breath short.

I'm getting scared, he whispered to himself.

And then he breathed out a long, low sigh.

Chapter

17

The bus pulled off the highway and stopped in front of a small supermarket to take on some passengers.

A man got on and went down the aisle and stopped by Ray.

"Mind if I sit here?"

"No," Ray said.

"Thanks."

He sat down in the aisle seat and the bus went back onto the highway and slowly picked up speed.

"It's beginning to snow," the man said.

He was in his forties, stocky and well-dressed.

"It's beginning to snow," he said again.

"Yes. It is."

"Think it will be a heavy one?"

Ray looked out the window at the leaden sky and the lazily falling snow. He shook his head.

"No. Looks like a light one to me."

"You from around here?"

"Yes," Ray said, and noted the slight scar on the man's cheek.

"I'm from the city. New York City."

"Oh."

"The Big Apple."

The man's voice was quiet and yet it had a hard quality to it. Almost a metallic undertone. His eyes were dark and melancholy.

"Thinking of finding a house around here and settling down."

"Uh-huh."

"I've two teenagers and I'm getting concerned."

"What about?"

"Crime. Too much crime in the city these days. It's becoming dangerous to walk the streets. Real dangerous."

Ray looked at the hard profile and smiled thinly.

"I guess it is."

He looked away from the man to the falling snow. They rode along silently for a while and then the man spoke again.

"How's crime up in these parts?"

"Not much," Ray said without turning.

I'm not going to see her, he said to himself. I'll do as she told me. I'll walk around town and then take the next bus back. I don't trust this guy. Don't trust him at all.

"How's the schools?"

"Schools?"

"You go to high school?"

"Just about finishing up."

"My daughter is in the second year. Is it a good school?"

Ray nodded.

"Yes. Pretty good."

"Education is very important these days. Very important."

"It always was," Ray said.

The man smiled but the eyes remained melancholy.

"True. I like you. What's your name?"

Ray hesitated.

"Mother tell you not to tell strangers your name? Mine's Pete Wilson."

"Ray Bond."

"Like in a Wall Street bond." The man laughed softly. "Good to meet you, Ray."

He put out his hand and they shook. His grip was firm and strong.

"I'm in trucking. What's your father in, Ray?"

Gambling, Ray was about to say bitterly.

"In nothing. He's dead."

"Oh. Sorry to hear that."

My uncle was a gambler, too, Ray wanted to shout at him. Come on, you know that, too. Sure you do. Stop putting me on.

But Ray turned silently away from the man and kept looking out at the steadily falling snow.

"You going to college?"

Ray turned back to him.

"It all depends," he said.

He looked into the harsh, melancholy eyes.

"Depends on what, Ray?"

On the thirty thousand dollars. You know that.

"Money?"

"Yes."

"It always does. Doesn't it?"

"Always," Ray said coldly.

"It's a hard world. No heart in it."

"Yes," Ray murmured.

"People live and die by the buck and for the buck. When I was a kid things were different. Very different."

He said the last words staring straight ahead of him. His face was tight and grim. The bus rode along into the oncoming dusk.

Wilson began to speak again, in a low and sad voice.

"I'm a religious person, Ray. That's how I was brought up and that's how I live and that's how I'm going to die. It pains me to see this going on all around me. We have no ethics. No ethics at all. We're losing our soul. We've made a jungle out of this beautiful world. And we're all savages. Real savages."

There was a flash of light from outside and it showed the little jagged scar on the man's face and then the light was gone and the man's face was in shadow again.

"Maybe it's good we'll all be blotted out by the

bomb. Maybe it's the best thing that will happen to us. We've lost our way. Lost it forever."

He didn't say another word until the bus started to pull into the outskirts of Louisville.

He turned to Ray.

"What town is this?"

"Louisville."

"Oh."

Ray sat there waiting for him to rise but Wilson stayed put in his seat.

"Aren't you getting off here?"

The man shook his head.

"What made you think that? I'm going to Chester."

"Chester?"

I was sure you were getting off here, Ray thought. To follow me. To see where I was going.

God, I was so sure of that.

"Got to see a real estate agent there. He's going to show me around the whole day tomorrow."

"Hope you find something."

"Thanks, Ray."

Ray rose and slid past the man and out into the aisle.

"So long, Ray. Be seeing you."

"So long."

"If I buy something around here I'll have my daughter look you up. If it's all right with you."

"Sure."

"I got to remember the name. Ray Bond."

"Like in a Wall Street bond."

"That's it."

They both laughed.

"She's real pretty. Takes after her mother. You'll like her."

"I'm sure I will."

"She's real intelligent. Has fine marks. Wants to be a scientist. What do you think of that?"

"She'll make it."

"You bet she will."

"So long, Mr. Wilson."

"Call me Pete. Everybody does."

They shook hands and Ray found himself liking the man.

"Luck, Pete," he said.

"I'll need it."

He walked down the aisle and paused when he came to the driver.

"Going shopping, Ray?"

Ray nodded. "Looking for a sweater."

And he said to himself, How quick and easy the lies come to me. How very quick.

"There's a sale on at Coleman's," the driver said.

"I'm heading there."

"Better get yourself a heavy sweater, Ray. The winter's here to stay a while."

"Looks like it."

"Take care, son."

"I'll try to."

Ray stepped out of the bus. The snow felt cool and soothing to his face and being.

He stood there watching the bus pull away from him and slowly disappear behind the veil of falling snow. The last thing he saw was the glowing red of the taillights. And then that, too, was blotted out. Only the veil of snow remained, and a silence that closed in about him.

"Take care," he murmured.

He stood there, thinking of the man on the bus, seeing his melancholy eyes again and hearing his voice.

We've lost our souls, our way. Lost it.

We've become savages. All of us.

I was fooled, Ray thought.

I could've sworn he was one of Dawson's men.

But he wasn't.

Ray turned and then started walking slowly to the hotel and as he walked the tension that lay within him now suddenly awoke and stirred violently.

The tension.

And the fear.

Chapter

18

He got out of the elevator and walked rapidly till he came to Room 418. He turned and looked back down the long, silent corridor and then he knocked on the door.

The sound of the knocking was the only sound.

He felt someone surveying him through the little round eye of the brass peephole. A cold tremor went through him.

"It's Ray Bond," he said and his voice was almost hoarse.

The door slowly opened and he saw the woman.

"Come in."

She took a quick, searching look down the silent, carpeted corridor and then drew back inside the room and closed the door behind him.

"You weren't followed?"

"No."

"You're sure? Absolutely sure?"

"Yes."

She sighed.

"Let me have your coat. It's wet from the snow."

"It's getting heavy out there," he said.

"I know. I was watching you through the window."

"Thought it was going to be a light one. But it's getting heavy."

"Yes," she said, her eyes scanning his taut face.

She put the coat on a wooden hanger and then motioned him to an easy chair. Then she came back into the room and sat down in a chair opposite him.

The room was large and neat. The blinds were drawn. There was an old glass ashtray near where she sat and he saw the stubs of crushed cigarettes, white under the dim lamplight.

Ray looked away from them and over to the woman.

Her face was pale and drawn.

"He knows you have the money. Doesn't he?" she said in a low voice.

Ray hesitated.

"Doesn't he?"

"I think so."

Her lips thinned. "Have you any idea how he found out?"

Ray shook his head. "No. I don't. I told nobody about it. Nobody. Not even my mother."

"Did he hint at it?"

"No."

"I've no idea how he knows. Ed was sure he would never find out. I would bet my life on it that Ed was sure." She sighed. "And he knows where the money is."

"I guess he does."

"Dawson knows." She smiled but her eyes were cold and bitter. "And now he wants the money back, doesn't he?"

Ray nodded.

"Yes."

"It's not his money. It's yours."

He stared at her. "But—"

She shook her head grimly. "It's yours. Ed paid him back."

"Are you sure?"

"I'm very sure."

Ray leaned forward to her. "Then why does Dawson come to me for the money?"

She didn't answer him.

"Why does he threaten me?"

She still didn't speak.

"He talks of killing me."

"He would."

"Says he'll kill me if I don't give him the money."

"I know."

She got up suddenly and went to the window and looked through the blinds to the street below.

She stood rigid and still.

He felt her tension come across the noiseless room and over to him.

"He's killed before," she said.

Then she let the slats of the blinds fall into place again and turned to him. Her shadow was upon the wall when she spoke. Her voice was sharp and unwavering.

"But he won't do it now."

"What do you mean?"

"I said he was paid back. Ed paid Dawson back with his life."

"I don't understand."

"You will."

She didn't speak for a while.

He sat there, studying her.

She was just above medium height, slender, with plain but straight features. Her hair was brown and her eyes hazel. She was at least in her mid-fifties. And the signs of oncoming age were beginning to appear in the lines about her eyes and on her pale forehead.

Her voice had a low and gentle quality to it but it could become hard and cold. Almost cutting.

She started to speak and her voice was now soft.

"I knew your uncle a long time. Knew him and loved him."

Ray didn't say anything.

"Loved him and also hated him."

"Hated?"

She looked straight at him, her eyes large and bright.

"Yes," she said. "Yes. That is the word."

"Why?"

She moved a few feet closer to him and then stopped.

"Why? It's simple. Live with a gambler and try not hating him. It's like . . . like living a life on a roller coaster. One day you have all the money and all you want. More than you ever could want. The next day you have nothing. Nothing but depression and dejection. And you both feel like jumping out of a window and ending it all."

Uncle Ed jumped out of a window and ended it all, he thought.

Twelve long dark stories.

Down, down, ever down, to smash his life out on a snowy pavement, on a snowy night like this one.

Just like this one.

Ray heard the woman's voice come softly and sadly over to him.

"Yet I can truly say, looking back on it all, that I loved him very much. I did, Ray. I did. Because all in all he tried to be a decent man. He tried his very heart out."

And failed, Ray thought.

"Tried. . . . He tried . . . again and again."

Her voice tightened and she turned her face away from him.

Ray thought of his mother and of how much

she hated his father. Without letup. Could she ever say that she had loved him? Say it as this woman just did of my uncle? No. I never heard Mom say one word that . . . not even a mumbling one.

Alice Cobb slowly came back to her chair and sat down again. She took out a cigarette and lit it. Her hands trembled just a bit as she blew out the tiny flame.

"I feel as if I'm your aunt. He often spoke to me about you."

"Did he?"

She nodded.

"Very often. A day didn't go by when he didn't talk about you and your hopes. Your wanting to be a lawyer."

"But I saw him so little," Ray said. "I wanted to see him more. To get close to him. Real close. He knew that. I'm sure he knew that."

"Yes," she said. "He did."

"Then why didn't he come around more? If he cared for me so much? Why didn't he?"

She looked over to him and her eyes were sad and pleading.

"He wanted so much to see you again and again. You've no idea how much he did, Ray."

"Then why?"

"You were his son, Ray. The son he never had."

"Why did he keep away? Why?"

She could not meet his eyes, she looked away from him.

"Ray, he was ashamed. Desperately ashamed of himself."

"What?"

"Yes. Yes. He never wanted you to find out what he was. You of all people. He wanted your respect. Your love."

Her voice trembled.

"Mine wasn't enough for him. He needed you. Needed you with all his lonely heart and soul. Do you understand that? Do you?"

Ray didn't answer.

"It would have been too painful to him if you did find out. Too devastating. He couldn't bear that. Not for a single moment. So the less he saw of you, the easier it was for him to keep up the deception."

"Didn't he ever try to cure his gambling?"

She shook her head.

"It didn't help. Just didn't work with him. It was in his bones. That's what he used to say wearily to me, 'It's in my bones, Alice. There to stay till the day I die.'"

"Skeleton man," Ray murmured.

"What?"

"He once said to my mother that he was a skeleton man. Do you know what he meant by that?"

"Skeleton man?"

"Yes."

"I think I do."

"Would you tell me?"

"I'll try."

He waited.

She lit another cigarette and then watched the flame of the match slowly die in the gleaming ashtray and then she spoke in a low but clear voice.

"What he meant was that he had emptied himself of all his humanity. The mad constant obsession to gamble had stripped him down to his very bones. Stripped him of everything that holds a person together. He could have been a fine and successful engineer. He had such a brilliant mind, particularly for mathematics. He could have been a . . . But he was nothing. Nothing at all."

She paused and then went on, her voice lowered almost to a whisper.

A haunting whisper.

"Skeleton man. He would never marry me and have children. He saw what had happened to his brother and to you. He never forgot that. Slowly but surely he became nothing but a skeleton man. He once said to me after he lost a lot of money at the casino, 'Alice, I died a long time ago. My skeleton drags on. I'm just a bunch of rattling bones. Just that and nothing more.' "

"He was wrong," Ray said.

It was hard for him to speak.

"Wrong. I could never have been ashamed of him. Never."

She was silent.

"I cared for him as much as he cared for me. More, I tell you. More."

She shook her head sadly.

"No, Ray. It couldn't have been more."

"Yes," he said.

His voice rose as he spoke.

"I loved him more than I did my own father. My own mother. More than even her. I did, I tell you."

She snuffed out her cigarette and stood up.

"Ray, he gave his life for you."

Ray stared at her.

"What do you mean?"

She drew in her breath and then spoke.

"I know this now. I didn't when he did it. Ray, he went to Dawson and borrowed that money knowing that he would never pay it back. He took the thirty thousand for you."

"For me," he whispered.

"Wouldn't dare losing it in a casino. The money was for you. To put into a bank vault and keep it there till you needed it."

He saw his uncle before him. Standing in the narrow room with the frosted glass door, the cold light overhead shining down upon them.

He heard her voice.

"Ray. In Dawson's world the penalty for not paying back money is death. Ed knew that."

She came close to him and stood there looking down at him.

Her face was white and taut. Like a mask. Only the eyes and the lips were alive.

"Ray, he never jumped from that window."

Ray waited.

"He was thrown out of it."

A great chill went through him and he trembled.

"Yes. That is what happened. It wasn't suicide. It was murder."

Murder.

He finally found his voice.

"How do you know this?"

"I know. Know it as well as I know that today is today."

"How?" he said again.

"I haven't the proof yet. But I'll get it. All that I need to take care of Dawson. Once and for all."

Her eyes glittered with hatred.

"He'll pay for Ed's murder. He will, Ray."

Her long narrow hands clenched and then unclenched.

"The suicide note," he said.

His eyes were ever on her.

"I wrote that note."

"You?"

She nodded.

"Why?"

She didn't answer him directly.

"I knew his handwriting and forged it."

"But why did you do it?"

She shook her head. "Someday when this is all over, I'll tell you."

Ray sat there looking at her.

Within him was a dark turmoil. Dark, fearful and chilling.

He heard her speak to him again.

"The money."

"Well?"

"You're not to give him one cent of that money. It's yours. Yours."

"But. . . ."

She cut in on him. "You're to use it for your education. Just as Ed wanted. Remember that. Always and always. Never lose sight of that truth. Your education."

"It's not my money," he said.

"Listen to me."

"It's Dawson's money. You admit it belongs to him."

She shook her head fiercely. "No. I told you it was paid back."

"No matter what you say, it is. . . ."

She cut in on him again, her eyes bright and flashing.

"Paid back with Ed's blood. His smashed body. His life. What more do you want? Why can't you see the truth of this? Why, Ray? Why can't you?"

She reached out and grabbed hold of his hand, her fingers tight about his wrist.

"You listen to me. You stall Dawson."

"What?"

"Do it. You can. He'll see you again. I know how he operates. He's patient. He waits. That's his style. Slow but sure. The violence comes last. But it will never come to you if you do as I ask."

"I can't do it."

Her grip tightened on his wrist. "You must."

"I just can't."

"I say you must. I need time. Just a little more time. And then everything will fall into place. Our way, Ray. Our way."

He didn't speak.

"Swear to me that you'll do it."

"I . . . I just . . . can't—"

And he couldn't go on.

She released his hand and went away from him over to the chair and then she slowly sat down again.

There was a silence. A cold, cold silence. He could almost feel the snow from outside come into the room.

He looked over to her. Her face had become slack and weary. Her body slumped in the chair.

"I guess you're right," she whispered. "You can't."

Ray barely heard her words.

He kept looking at her and suddenly she became old to him. Old and beaten.

"It's no use," she whispered.

He felt a great surge of pity for her. Pity and a desperate warmth.

My aunt.

She said that.

I'll bet I'm all she has left in this world.

Her only nephew.

That's all Uncle Ed had.

Me.

Then he heard her speak again, in a low and heartbreaking voice.

"Ed gave his life for you."

"I know," he murmured.

"He did, Ray. You must believe me."

"I believe you," he said.

But she didn't seem to hear him.

"I'm putting my life on the line, too."

She is, he thought to himself.

"Are you aware of that?"

"Yes."

She looked up and then across the room to him.

"Do you want it all to be for nothing?"

He didn't answer her.

"Do you?"

He sighed low.

"All right," he said. "I'll try it your way."

Then he saw the tears come to her eyes.

"Your way," he said again.

"He won't harm you. I swear that to you."

"I know."

But he didn't believe her.

When he left, the tears were still in her eyes.

Chapter

19

He was sitting in class trying to keep his mind on what Mr. Wallace was saying when his eyes strayed over to where Laurie was sitting.

He gazed yearningly at the back of her head, at her softly glowing hair.

Then she turned as if she were aware of his looking at her.

Her eyes smiled gently at him.

He smiled back to her.

And within him a great peace descended.

He listened intently to what Mr. Wallace was saying and he understood each word now.

But then he turned for some reason to glance out of the window to the white snow and bare trees and he saw the figure standing against one of the gray oak trees.

Tall in a tight-fitting blue coat. With a tan felt hat.

Just standing there.

Like a death.

Chapter

20

He was lying in the cold darkness, his eyes open, thinking, ever thinking, when he heard his mother come silently into the room.

She stood there, in the shadows, gazing at him.

"Are you still up, Ray?"

She spoke in a soft, anxious voice.

"Yes."

"I can't sleep," she said.

That makes two, he thought wearily.

"Can I talk to you?"

"If you want."

He heard her sit down on a chair near his desk.

"I feel that something is wrong," she said.

Everything is wrong, Mother.

Every thing.

"You're not yourself, Ray."

"I'm all right."

"You don't talk much anymore."

"I never talked much," he said.

"There's something on your mind."

"There always is."

"No. This time it's different."

"Try to sleep, Mom. There's nothing wrong."

"It's a feeling. A deep one."

"Forget it."

She got up and came close to him.

"Is everything all right between you and Laurie?"

"Yes, Mom. Go to sleep."

"You haven't quarreled?"

"No."

"The truth?"

"Yes."

"I like Laurie very much but she has a temper."

"That's one of her good features."

"She's Irish, isn't she?"

"Scotch-Irish."

"That's a combination."

"I like the combination," he said.

"Then everything's all right with the two of you?"

"Couldn't be better. Good night, Mom."

But she still stood there.

"Maybe I shouldn't have told you about your father. Maybe it's that."

"It isn't."

"Then what is it?"

"Nothing. It's nothing."

"Please tell me."

He looked through the darkness at her and there was a great ache in his heart.

I never could, Mom. Not in a thousand years. We live in two different worlds. So terribly different. You won't understand me. And I won't understand you.

That's how it is.

That's how it always was.

That's how it will be.

Ever and ever.

He heard his mother's voice come to him, sad and determined.

"It's your father. That's what it is."

"No."

"I shouldn't have told you about him. I swore to myself you'd never know the shame he brought to us."

He turned to her. "Mom."

"Yes?"

"I'm not ashamed of my father."

She didn't speak.

"I feel sorry for him. So awfully sorry."

"I don't," she said.

"I know that."

"I had to move from the town we were living in. Find a new place for us. He was never a father to you, and as a husband to me he was the—"

Ray cut in softly.

"Mom. Let him rest where he is. Please."

Her face was pale in the darkness.

"I'm sorry, Ray."

Then they both were silent.

A slight breeze crept through the barely opened window and the curtain swirled and then gradually came to rest when the breeze died away.

"Mom," he said. "I remember something. Young as I was then I remember it now."

"What, Ray?"

He paused and then went on in a low, searching voice.

"I sat with you in a courtroom and a man looked at me and there was such a sadness in his face. His eyes were so . . . so . . . pleading . . . pleading with me. . . . With me—"

His voice trailed off into the darkness.

"Your father," she said.

"Ah," he whispered.

The curtain began to swirl again, softly.

He began to speak.

"Maybe it was then. Maybe then . . . it may have started within me—"

He didn't go on.

"What, Ray?"

He sighed and then spoke again.

"To become a lawyer and help people with the sad faces and lost, lonely eyes."

"It was then?"

He nodded.

"I'm sure of it. Young as I was."

"The lost people," she said in a low voice.

"They need help. And there's so many of them. So many, Mom."

"There are."

They both looked through the darkness and saw each other's face.

For the first time in his entire life he felt very close to her, closer than he had ever been.

And then the moment slipped away from him.

"Go to sleep, Mom," he finally said in a gentle voice.

"All right, Ray."

She bent low and kissed him on the forehead.

Then he heard her go out of his room.

He lay in bed, for a long while, wondering when Dawson would call again.

His eyes closed and he slept.

21

He dreamt of his father.

He was sitting in a cell, next to his father.

The sun came through the window and made barred shadows on the cement floor.

Ray kept looking at the barred shadows. His face tight and grim.

"You didn't," he said.

"I tried my best, Ray."

Ray shook his head.

"You left us poor and alone."

"I didn't mean to."

"Mom works hard for practically nothing. And I have to work and worry about money to keep the house going and to go on to college."

"I stole for you, Ray."

"You didn't."

"I swear on my soul."

"You have no soul."

"Don't say that to me. Please don't."

"I don't believe a word you tell me. Not a word."

His father put his arm about Ray's shoulder.

"I love you, Ray. I did it for you."

"You're lying."

"Ray."

"You are. All gamblers are liars."

The hand fell away from his shoulder.

"Why do you say that to me?"

"Because it's the truth."

His father's voice almost broke.

"Why are you so cruel to me?"

"Because you were cruel to Mom and me."

"I tell you I tried."

"And I tell you you're lying."

His father suddenly rose and shouted for the guard.

"Leave me," he said to Ray. "Don't torture me anymore."

"Okay."

Ray got up and walked to the metal door and the guard opened it for him and just as Ray was about to step into the noisy corridor he heard his father's voice.

"You're right, Ray. You're so right. I stole to gamble. That's all it was. To gamble."

Ray turned to him and there were tears on his father's face.

Then Ray woke up and there were tears on his face.

He wiped them away with his hand.

And began thinking again of Dawson.

Chapter

22

Albert Dawson did call.

He seemed to know when Ray would be alone in the house. When the ring of the phone would be sudden, clear and startling.

Ray stood there, holding the receiver with a tight grip, and listening to the man's smooth, precise voice.

"I'd like to see you, Ray."

"I know. I was waiting for you."

"I thought you would be."

Outside the sky was beginning to darken and the long shadows to fall near the silent trees, dark and almost blue against the whiteness of the snow. All was quiet and still and hovering.

He picks his time so accurately, Ray thought grimly, like a cunning stage director of a horror play.

The curtain goes up on a silent, shadowy room.
The phone rings. Cold and clear.
The audience begins to shiver with expectation.
A murder will soon be done. Blood will flow.
How theatrical this all is . . . and yet how real.
How deadly real to me.

"When do you want to see me?" Ray asked.

His voice sounded so calm to him, so very calm,
while within he trembled.

"I have to be in Atlantic City tomorrow. So
that's out."

"Collecting money?"

"Yes. How did you know?"

"What else do you do with your life but that?"
Dawson laughed softly.

"Quite true. Make it the day after tomorrow."

"All right."

"So it's the day after. We're set."

"We are."

And Ray thought to himself, just a short time
ago this man meant absolutely nothing to me, as if
he had never existed.

Now he is my life. Or my death.

"What time, Dawson?"

"Afternoon. Would that be convenient?"

"Yes."

"Three o'clock?"

"All right."

"You're certain it's convenient? I don't want to
interfere with your school activities."

"You're not."

The shadows by the trees deepened just a bit.

"Good. I understand you're an excellent student."

"You've been asking around."

"Of course."

"In your quiet way."

"Quiet and unobtrusive."

"You have your own beautiful and patented style, don't you, Mr. Dawson," Ray said sardonically.

Again he heard the man's soft laugh.

"I should, Ray. It took me years to develop it."

Years and how many beaten and dead victims? Ray thought grimly.

"Where do you want to see me?" he said aloud.

"Why not the bench?"

"All right."

"Come alone."

"I will."

Then Ray heard the click.

He thought of Alice Cobb and at that moment, that single, precise moment, he found himself hating her.

I never should have given her my word, he said to himself bitterly.

Never.

I should give the man back his blood-soaked money and be done with this.

Done.

And then I would begin to breathe again.

Chapter

23

He was walking along the deserted sidewalk in the gray afternoon, when he felt that a car was following him, following him slowly, and then just after he passed the town's police station, he heard his name called softly. Softly and clearly.

"Ray Bond?"

He trembled slightly and turned around.

"As in a Wall Street bond."

The car pulled over to the curb and stopped.

The driver opened the door and came out and over to him, his hand outstretched.

"I thought it was you."

Ray silently shook the strong hand and looked into the dark and melancholy eyes of Pete Wilson.

They were smiling now, smiling and yet quietly observing him.

"How're you doing, Ray?"

"All right."

"Life's on a steady keel since I last saw you?"

"I guess so."

He felt uneasy meeting Wilson again. He didn't know why.

"I couldn't find anything in the other town. Spent a whole day there in the snow. Found nothing I thought I would like."

"Sorry to hear that."

"Don't be. I've been looking around here again and I think I have something lined up."

Ray looked at a little, jagged scar on the man's rough-featured face and didn't say anything.

"Maybe you can help me out, Ray."

"How?"

"There's a house I'm interested in. It's on Clark and Elm."

"Oh."

"You know where it is? You should."

"Yes."

"I want to take another look at it. How about the neighborhood? It looks pretty decent to me."

"It is," Ray said.

I can't make you out, Ray thought, there's something about you. . . .

"How far is it from the high school?"

"About half a mile."

"Then my daughter can walk it in good weather?"

"I think so."

"Ray, how about coming along with me?"

"I have something to do, Mr. Wilson."

But he didn't.

"Pete. I told you to call me Pete."

"Pete."

The man smiled. But the melancholy eyes still probed into Ray, the dark, melancholy eyes.

"Come on, Ray. A few minutes of your time. Help me a lot. You'll tell me more about the neighborhood."

Ray was about to shake his head but Wilson put his arm affectionately about his shoulder.

"Help out a pal. Will you?"

And for some strange reason, Ray thought of the dream he had last night and of his father's beseeching arm about his shoulder. And of how cruel he had been to the man.

"How about it, Ray?"

Ray hesitated.

"What is it? Something bugging you?"

The arm was still about his shoulder, warm and friendly.

"It's nothing," Ray said.

He slowly got into the car.

Chapter

24

They rode along for a while, not speaking to each other, and then Wilson reached over and patted Ray on the knee.

"Relax. You're with a friend."

"What?"

"You're all tensed up about something."

"I'm okay."

"What is it, Ray?"

"Nothing. Nothing at all."

Wilson glanced over to him.

"I saw you walking toward the police station. Anything wrong?"

Ray shook his head.

"I was passing it."

"Not going in?"

"Why should I go in?"

Wilson shrugged and smiled.

"That's what I'm asking."

He stopped the car for a red light.

"Ever think of police stations?"

"Think of them? How?"

"I have. A lot. My philosophy is this, Ray. Police stations are sometimes good for you and sometimes bad."

"Why bad, Mr. Wilson?"

Wilson shook a finger at Ray.

"I told you to call me Pete."

"Pete."

The man laughed softly and drove on.

"Police stations," he said. "I told you I'm in trucking. And that can be a very rough business. You know anything about long-haul trucking?"

"No."

"Things come up. Bad things. And sometimes I have to go to the police station to help straighten things out." He paused and looked at Ray. "And sometimes I stay away from it."

"Why?"

Wilson's eyes hardened.

"I told you on the bus that life can be a jungle. Do you remember?"

"I remember," Ray murmured.

"When people become savage then you have to take on jungle ways. Because that's the only way you're going to survive."

He made a sudden turn of the steering wheel and the car entered a lonely, tree-lined lane.

"This is not the way to Elm Road," Ray said.

"I know."

Ray stared silently at the grim profile of the man.

"I want to have a private talk with you."

Wilson stopped the car under the thick and bare branches of a huge plane tree. Then he quietly turned to Ray.

Ray looked into the man's dark, hard eyes and a chill of terror went through him.

He heard Wilson speak.

"Sometimes you have to straighten things out for yourself. Do you know what I mean?"

Wilson flipped open his jacket and Ray saw a shoulder holster with the butt of a gun staring out of it, stark and black. He was mesmerized by the cold menace of the gun.

"That's what I mean, Ray."

"You're with Dawson, aren't you?"

"No. Who's he?"

You're lying, Ray said to himself. You always were. You fooled me on the bus.

"What about this fellow Dawson?"

"You tell me."

"Don't know him from a hole in the ground."

"I'm sure of it."

Wilson closed his jacket and the gun was blotted out of view.

"I can feel you're in some trouble, Ray. I can smell trouble. That's why I'm speaking to you."

"To help me."

"That's right."

"You like me an awful lot, don't you?" Ray said bitterly.

"I said I did, didn't I?"

"Sure."

The man's eyes suddenly became somber.

"So listen to me. Stay away from police stations."

Ray was silent.

"It will only bring you a lot of grief. Believe me, I know."

"I'll bet you do."

"You going to stay away from them?"

Ray slowly nodded.

"You'll promise me?"

Or else you'll use that gun on me, Ray thought hopelessly.

"Well?"

"Yes," Ray said.

Wilson suddenly smiled, a warm, gentle smile.

"You're making me feel a lot better now, Ray. I know you're going to keep your word."

He patted Ray on the knee and then reached over and opened the car door.

"You can walk home from here. It's not far."

"What about the house you're buying?" Ray asked sardonically.

"We'll see it another day. Just you and I."

Ray silently stepped out of the car.

"I'm your friend, Ray. Always remember that."

Then Ray watched the car back up and out of the lane. It turned and caught a glint of the pale sun and then he no longer saw it.

Chapter

25

He opened the oblong metal box and saw the medal lying on the green, crisp thousand dollar bills.

He picked up the medal and put it aside.

Then he took out the bills, one by one, and counted them.

Thirty thousand dollars.

He opened a white envelope and slowly put the money into it.

I'm through, he said to himself. I'm on my way to see Dawson. I'm handing the money over to him and that's the end of it all. The end.

He was about to put the envelope with the money into his inner jacket pocket when his eyes rested on the glinting medal.

And he saw again the man and the night and

heard again the man's heart-breaking voice against the sound of the dark ocean.

They stripped me clean.

Clean.

I want to go home.

Home.

Just to go home.

And then he saw the eyes of his dead uncle as he lay flat and silent on the snowy sidewalk. The haunting, pleading eyes, no longer smiling. Never to smile again.

And he heard again the voice of the slender, brown-haired woman.

Ray, he paid the debt. Paid it with his life.

With his broken body.

For you.

For you to go on and be what you want to be.

"I can't do it," Ray said.

He took the money out of the envelope and laid it back into the box, bill by bill.

Then he took the medal and placed it on top of the bills. Gently. So very gently.

He closed the box.

And handed it to the attendant.

Chapter

26

As he came out of the bank and into the chill, wintry air, he saw Laurie standing on the sidewalk, as if waiting for him.

He went over to her.

"You've been following me," he said curtly.

"Yes."

"Why?"

"Why'd you go into the bank?"

"To make a deposit. What's wrong in that?"

"You went down into the vault room."

"How do you know?"

"I went in and saw you go down there."

"So?"

"So you tell me."

He looked angrily at her.

"I don't like this, Laurie. It's none of your business."

"I'm making it my business."

"Then don't."

"What's down there? Down in that vault box?"

"Nothing."

"I feel that your trouble has something to do with that box."

"You feel wrong."

"What is it? Tell me."

"Nothing."

Her hair swung back and her eyes flashed fiercely at him.

"Always nothing."

"Yes."

"That's a crock," she said bitterly.

"So it's a crock."

Her voice rose when she spoke again.

"Nothing. That's your favorite expression whenever somebody questions you. I've heard it for years whenever you want to clam up. Nothing, Laurie. Nothing and again nothing."

She turned away from him angrily and stepped off the curb.

"Laurie."

He suddenly reached over and pulled her back and out of the path of an oncoming car.

"Watch yourself," he said grimly.

"You watch yourself."

"You could've been killed."

And as he said that, a throb of fear for her went through him.

"So?"

He didn't say anything.

They stepped back onto the curb and waited for the light to change.

"Laurie," he said in a gentle voice. "I told you to stay out of this."

"I know what you told me. Know it well enough."

"Then do what I say."

"No."

"I want you to."

"And I want you to tell me what is wrong. What trouble you're in."

The light changed and they crossed the street without saying a word to each other.

When they got to the other side she turned to him.

"Well?"

He looked wearily at her.

"I said once, you're beating a dead horse and now you're doing it again."

"Because you're your stubborn self again."

"I'm not."

"You are. You have no feeling for me. None at all. You never had."

"Never?"

"Yes. Never."

"How can you say that to me?"

"I'm saying it. Loud and clear."

"Laurie."

"Oh, stop it."

"Okay," he said grimly.

Then he turned abruptly away from her and started walking down a deserted side street.

She swiftly followed and then caught up with him.

"Ray."

He stopped and turned to her.

"Well?" she said.

He didn't speak. They stood there, alone and apart. Just the two of them.

Laurie, he thought to himself. Laurie.

His eyes pleaded desperately with her when he spoke.

"You shouldn't say those bitter things to me, Laurie. You shouldn't. I have such a deep feeling for you. You know that in your heart."

"Sure."

"That's why I want you to stay out of this."

"You're thinking of me."

"Yes."

"To protect me."

"That's it, Laurie."

"I appreciate it."

He leaned close to her and he thought for an instant that she would relent and kiss him, he so much wanted her to, but suddenly she pushed him back and away from her.

Her voice rang out. "I don't want your protection. Stop giving me this macho stuff. It turns my stomach."

"Laurie."

"I'm well able to take care of myself."

"Not in this."

"I am, I tell you."

"You don't know what this is all about."

"Because you're clamming up like you always do."

He sighed and stood there looking at her, at her hair blowing in the soft wind, at her clear eyes, sharp and bright with anger and yet on the point of tears, and he thought to himself, Why do we always have to hurt the people we care about? The people we love. Why?

Why does it always come out this way?

Why?

He heard her voice come through to him.

"Well? Are you going to tell me?"

His lips thinned to a tight line.

"Laurie," he said. "Stay out of this. Don't ever follow me again. If you do I'll never speak to you. Never again."

He saw her face go pale and stricken, as if he had struck her. His heart felt sick and heavy within him.

Then he turned and walked silently away from her.

Chapter

27

When he came there the man was sitting on the wooden bench and then he saw the gray cat sitting under the tree sunning itself in the pale winter sun.

A man in a dark blue coat and a large gray cat. Both motionless. Like statues.

Ray never forgot that sight as long as he lived. Never.

Nor what happened later.

He went over to the bench and sat down without a word.

"You have a pleasant day, Ray?"

"Very," Ray said.

"It shows on your face."

"I'll bet it does."

Dawson smiled a thin smile.

"And you've been sleeping well?"

"Yes."

"No dreams? No nightmares?"

"None."

"Can I believe you?"

"If you want."

Dawson shook his head. "I don't, Ray."

"Then you don't."

Dawson took his pipe out of his coat pocket and then filled the pipe from a black leather pouch. All the time his eyes were studying Ray's grim profile.

He finally spoke.

"Been thinking over what we talked about the last time?"

"I have."

"Good."

Dawson lit his pipe and then looked out ahead of him. The field was empty, flat and empty, and here and there were patches of white snow. Above, the sky was clear and blue. All about them was a great and wide silence.

"I understand you went to see Alice Cobb," Dawson said quietly.

Ray turned sharply to him.

"What?"

Dawson smiled.

"You did, didn't you?"

Then I was followed, Ray thought bitterly, and I told her I wasn't.

"Well?"

It must've been Wilson, Pete Wilson. He never went on to the next town. Got off the bus a minute after I did and then followed me.

"You haven't answered me, Ray."

"Do I have to?"

"Perhaps not."

The cat stirred and then lay down gracefully and extended its long smooth body, its large head resting on its gray paws. Ray could now see its eyes. They were green, pale, glittering green.

"A most unusual-looking cat, isn't it?"

Ray was silent.

"Sleek and beautiful and strange."

The cat's eyes were round and staring—ever staring at the two of them. Coldly. Impassively.

"I found him here as if waiting for me. Sent by destiny."

Then Dawson said something that Ray never forgot.

"I believe he'll come in useful later on."

Ray felt a chill spread through him.

"Quite useful. To help make a point. Do you follow me?"

"No."

"Then you will. As your excellent teacher Mr. Wallace says, In time everything becomes quite clear. In time. That's the history and hope of science."

"How do you know he says that?"

"He does, doesn't he?"

"Yes."

"I know, Ray, because it's my business to know."

There was a glitter of mockery in the man's eyes. And then it went away and the man spoke again.

"What did the woman say to you?"

"Nothing much."

"Tell me," Dawson said gently.

"She lived with my uncle and she wanted to see me."

"Why?"

"To give me a watch of his. An old pocket watch."

"A gold case, no doubt."

Ray nodded silently.

"Gave it to you as a memento."

"Yes."

Dawson smiled but his blue eyes were cold and appraising.

"She did live with your uncle. But only at times."

"What do you mean?"

"Alice Cobb was and is a sick woman. Did you know that?"

Ray didn't answer.

"An emotionally sick woman. She was away for treatment time and time again."

"I don't believe you."

"I didn't expect you to."

Ray looked away from him to the silent and open field.

"She lived with a gambler. He made her sick."

And Ray remembered the words she had said to him. It's like living on a roller coaster. You're up one day. The next day you're down. Way, way down.

He heard Dawson's soft and precise voice come through to him.

"You can't put much faith in what she tells you, Ray. The woman is full of fantasies. All the time. I know, my boy."

The cat turned its large sleek head and stared directly at Ray. Only at Ray. As if trying to probe through to his very heart.

Ray felt a shiver go through him. As if he could see what was going to happen. He felt a sudden urge to get up and run away from it all.

Then he heard Dawson's voice.

"Fantasies. Your uncle did not commit suicide. She told that to you, didn't she?"

Ray turned away from the piercing, hypnotic eyes of the cat and back to Dawson.

"No," he said.

"Of course she did. What else did she say?"

"You tell me. You seem to know it all."

Dawson paused to relight his pipe and then he spoke again.

"She said that your uncle was thrown out of the hotel window. Didn't she?"

"No."

"That he was murdered."

"No, I tell you. Leave her out of this. She told me nothing."

Dawson shook his head slowly.

"Listen to me, Ray. She's wrong. Absolutely wrong. At that time I did not know that your uncle had turned the money over to you. He had been late with his payments in the past and I thought he would come up with this one."

Ray was silent.

"I'm speaking the truth."

"You were going to give him time?"

"Yes."

"I don't believe you."

"You must. I swear to you I gave it to him in the past. Why not now?"

Ray didn't answer.

The truth, he said to himself. Where is the truth?

He heard Dawson's voice.

"I was going to give him time. But then he jumped out of the window. Jumped, I tell you."

You're lying, Ray thought.

Or are you?

Where is the truth? Where?

He felt Dawson's gloved hand on his arm.

He turned to him.

"Ray, listen to me. I never lie. I tell things as they are. I have no illusions about you or anybody else in this harsh life of ours. Least of all do I have illusions about myself."

He paused and went on.

"I act only out of necessity. Only that. That is the iron law of my life."

The grip tightened on Ray's arm.

"There was no necessity for me to have your uncle killed. None whatsoever. Not at that time."

"But later on?"

"If he had not paid?"

"Yes."

"You know the answer."

The hand relaxed its grip, but it still held Ray's arm.

"Then you did not have him killed?" Ray said.

"No."

"But you've had other people killed?"

The man answered without hesitation.

"When it was necessary."

Ray looked hard at the man.

"You are honest, aren't you?"

"That is all I have left. Honesty, Ray."

"What do you mean by that?"

Dawson shook his head and slowly took his hand away from Ray's arm.

"There's no point in going into that," he said bleakly.

They both were silent, looking away from each other. The cat still lay there, motionless, staring directly at Ray, its green eyes glittering.

"Only by necessity," Ray said quietly. "So what you're saying to me is, that if I don't come up with the money. . . ."

"I'm saying that time is running out on you. Fast."

"I understand."

Neither spoke.

A soft, wintry wind blew over the desolate field and rustled the silky hairs of the gray, motionless cat. Dawson tapped the bowl of his pipe against the wood of the bench and then put the pipe away in his coat pocket. And it was then, and only then, that Ray noticed the slight bulge in the other pocket of the dark blue coat.

"Is that a gun?" Ray asked pointing to the pocket.

"Yes," the man said gently. "A gun with a silencer. I keep it for protection."

"Against whom?"

"One never knows."

Ray looked away from the man and out to the desolate field.

We're alone, he thought. So completely alone.

"You would have me killed," Ray said in a low voice.

"I'm afraid I would."

"And yet I feel that you like me."

"I do."

"Do you have any sons?"

"None, Ray. I am alone."

"And if you had sons. Even one. Would you still kill me?"

"I'm hoping and thinking that you'll give me the money. In fact, I believe that you will and that we'll part as friends, if that is possible."

"You haven't answered my question."

"If I had a son?"

"If you had a son my age. Would you still kill me?"

"I've no doubt that I would."

Ray looked at him, at the quiet, impassive face, at the cold blue eyes, and something within him snapped and suddenly he cried out in a harsh and bitter voice.

"You asked me how I sleep? Do I have dreams? Nightmares? How do you sleep? How?"

Dawson's face paled.

"How can you go on doing what you do?"

"I am what I've become," Dawson said curtly. "Let it go at that."

They both were standing now, facing each other.

"Tell me," Ray shouted. "Tell me how does a human being turn into an animal? I want to know. I have to know so I can sleep nights."

"We're through talking, Ray."

"Tell me."

Ray grabbed him by his coat and the man flung him off.

"I let you get too close to me," Dawson said savagely. "Much too close."

He swung about as if to go away and then he seemed to get hold of himself and he turned slowly back to Ray.

His face was now ashen but taut and composed, his voice low and controlled.

"I forgot the lesson," he said.

The gun was out of his pocket and in his hand.

"I'm about to make a point, Ray."

"No," Ray whispered.

He stood there, rooted to the spot, unable to move.

"Just as Mr. Wallace does in his classes. An object lesson."

"Don't do it. Please."

The cat lay there staring at them. But something new had come into its eyes. A look of fear. And yet it didn't move from the spot. Just lay there looking directly at them. As if, like Ray, it was held there by its destiny.

"Watch closely," Dawson said in a flat, emotionless voice.

"Please."

Ray raised his hand toward the man.

But it was too late. There was a hiss of the bullet, the impact, the cat shivered and was still.

Dawson turned to Ray.

"The next time I talk to you it will be to tell you where to deliver the money."

A surge of fury swept through Ray.

"You'll never get it," he shouted. "You'll kill me first."

"I'll get it. You'll bring it to me."

Then Ray saw the man walk away from him and slowly and gradually disappear from his sight.

Leaving him alone on the desolate field.

So utterly alone.

Chapter

28

It was eleven o'clock at night. He lay in bed sleeping. His mother had not yet come home.

He began to dream.

He suddenly found himself in the middle of a casino, standing at a slot machine, and around him was a crowd of excited onlookers.

He pulled the lever and there was a gasp from the crowd.

"He's won again."

"He's on a streak."

"A miracle streak."

"He'll empty out the casino of all its money."

"He's the luckiest kid I ever saw."

"He'll need an armored truck to take the money away."

"No. They'll give him a certified bank check."

"Is that what they do?"

And Ray suddenly turned on them all and shouted, his voice echoing throughout the entire casino. All activity stopped and everyone listened to him in stunned silence.

"I don't want this money. It's blood money. You're all fools. Dupes. You come here and give them your hard-earned salaries, your little savings, and you dump it all into these robber machines and you never win. And if you win you give it back. You always give it back. Don't you?"

Then he turned and pushed his way through the startled and still silent people and there was Dawson standing in his path.

"Go back, Ray. Go back and play some more."

"I don't want to."

"Go back and win some more."

"No."

"You're a good example to those pigeons. We let you win so they can have their dreams and their illusions. What is life without dreams and illusions? It's a crock, don't you think?"

"It's a crock," Ray smiled.

He began to laugh, while tears streamed from his eyes, tears of bitterness and of sorrow.

And Dawson laughed with him, but there were no tears in his eyes.

"It's a crock," they both sang out.

Then Dawson affectionately put his arm about Ray and they both began to dance down the aisle and the people all about them began to sing.

Life is a crock.

A crock.

A crock.

And it was then that Ray awoke and heard the insistent ringing of the telephone.

He got out of bed and went downstairs to answer it.

Chapter

29

He picked up the phone.

"Ray?"

It was Alice Cobb.

"Yes?"

"Ray, I've got what I was looking for. I've got it, Ray. I've got it."

Her voice was taut, excited, almost gay. It made him tremble just a bit. The dream was still with him. The hallway was dim and cold.

"Where are you?" he asked.

"In my hotel room. Listen to me. You must come to see me. Now."

"Now? It's late at night."

"Is it? Oh, I forgot. Yes, you're right. Then tomorrow."

"Dawson knows that you—"

She laughed bitterly and cut in on him.

"I don't care what Dawson knows. I don't care anymore. He's the one in danger now, not me."

He wondered if she had been drinking.

"Miss Cobb," he said.

"Call me Alice. Better still, call me Aunt Alice."

"Are you all right?"

"What do you mean?"

"You sound a bit—"

He didn't go on.

"I've had a few drinks, if that's what you mean. I'm high. I'm flying. Because we've won, Ray, we've won."

He was silent. He looked through the window and out at the night sky. A wind shook the branches of the winter trees.

"Are you there?" Her voice was quieter now, more in control.

"Yes."

"I'm sorry. I must've let myself go. It's just that . . . well, you know what I mean, Ray."

"I do," he said.

But he didn't.

"I've had some drinks," she said. "I'm too charged up. I shouldn't have called you at this hour. But I just had to. I had to, Ray."

"Sure."

"Ray, you must come and see me. Did I tell you that?"

"Yes."

"I want you to have a copy of the evidence. So if anything happens to me you'll have it."

"What evidence?"

"What do you mean what evidence?"

Her voice was almost hostile now.

"Just what I said."

"The evidence that Ed never jumped."

"Oh."

The wind shook the bare branches again and it made him feel colder and more insecure.

"Where did you get it?" he asked.

"Where?"

"Yes, where?"

He was getting angry and weary of her.

"In Ed's hotel room, of course."

Maybe Dawson spoke the truth, he said to himself. Maybe she is a sick woman.

"But the police searched the room, didn't they?"

"So did I."

"And?"

"This time I found it."

"Found what?"

"What I was looking for."

He controlled his voice.

He spoke quietly.

"Could you tell me what it is?"

"Not on the phone. I have to see you. I have diagrams I've made."

"Diagrams?"

"Yes. Why do you question me so? What's wrong with you, Ray?"

He sighed. "Alice," he said.

"Aunt Alice."

And he suddenly thought of Pete Wilson. . . .

Call me Pete. Pete.

He heard her voice.

"What were you going to say? Tell me."

He didn't answer her.

"I think I know," she said.

"Well?"

"You've seen Dawson and spoken to him again."

"I saw him."

"And you discussed me."

"He said some things about you."

"I know exactly what he said."

She laughed harshly and was silent.

He waited for her to speak again.

"He told you I was mentally ill. A psycho."

"Something like that," he said.

Why did I say that to her, he thought to himself. Why am I so cruel to her?

And then he heard her voice, low and vulnerable.

"Dawson is telling the truth on that one."

His hands quivered.

"I've had my downs. A lifetime of them with Ed. I am a psycho."

And suddenly he felt sorry for her.

"But I'm in control now and my mind is as clear as a bell. I tell you that Dawson murdered your uncle. I know it for a fact, Ray."

Is it a fact, Aunt Alice, he thought wearily, or some wild fantasy of yours?

"It is a fact, Ray," she said, as if she had heard his silent words.

And then she spoke again, almost curtly, as though she had been insulted and bitterly resented it.

"I know it's a fact. Know it. But there's no point in going into this now."

"I guess there isn't."

There was a slight pause.

"Will you come to see me?"

He hesitated. "Well, I. . . ."

"Please. You must."

He saw his mother come out of the night and onto the porch and then approach the front door of the house.

"Tomorrow, Ray. The same time as the last time."

That's the name of a song, he thought to himself. The words and tune came to him. The same time as the last time. The same ti. . . .

"Will you, Ray?"

Now she was pleading desperately with him.

"All right," he sighed.

"Goodbye, Ray."

"Goodbye," he said.

He hung up just as his mother came into the dark house.

"Ray?"

He looked through the darkness to her.

"A wrong number," he said.

"Oh."

"Woke me out of my sleep."

And then he turned and went up the staircase, slowly, very slowly.

Conscious of her eyes upon him.

Chapter

30

There was no one sitting next to him this time. And when the bus came to his stop he went up to the driver. He nodded to him and turned to the open door.

"Ray."

Ray looked back to the driver.

"You know, the other night when you were on this bus?"

"Yes?"

"The night you went in to buy a sweater?"

"Uh-huh."

"That fellow you were sitting with and talking to?"

"I remember."

"Well, he acted kind of strange."

"What do you mean?"

"He comes up to me just a few seconds after you got off and he says to me, 'Please let me off now.'"

"He did?"

"I thought he was going on to the next town."

"That's what he told me."

The driver shook his head.

"Stepped down and then seemed to go right after you. In a hurry."

So Wilson did follow me to the hotel, Ray thought grimly. But he's nowhere around now. Nor anybody else.

Ray smiled bleakly at the driver and stepped off the bus.

"Take care of yourself, Ray."

"I'll try to."

And then he turned and walked slowly through the oncoming night, a sense of foreboding heavy within him.

Chapter

31

He went down the long, silent corridor till he came to Room 418. He knocked on the door, looking about him all the time. He was alone.

He knocked again and waited for her to come to the brass peephole.

But no one came.

There was only the dull silence of the corridor.

He knocked a third time.

Again no answer.

He put his ear to the door and heard the muffled ringing of the telephone coming from within. It rang again and again. But no one answered it.

Finally, the ringing stopped.

Again, the silence.

He looked at his watch.

Five thirty.

Ray put his hand to the doorknob and the door swung slowly and silently open.

He felt a cold thrill go through him.

He hesitated on the threshold and then stepped into the room.

"Alice?"

His voice sounded gray and hollow in the empty room.

He turned and closed the door behind him and went further into the room. Everything was neat and in perfect order. Except the ashtray.

The ashtray, as before, was full of cigarette stubs.

The blinds were drawn.

The lamp by the window was on, casting a shadow on the blank wall. Large and dark and precisely outlined, as if cut out with the gleaming blade of a sharp, a very sharp, knife.

Then suddenly the phone rang and startled him.

He stood there staring at it.

The ringing stopped.

He felt his knees shaking, so he went over to a chair and slowly sat down.

There was an icy sweat on his forehead.

His hands were hot and clammy.

Something is wrong, he said to himself. Something is terribly wrong.

Then the phone rang again.

He got up slowly and went over to it.

The cold, black receiver mesmerized him. He kept looking down at it and then suddenly he found it in the grip of his hand and the sound of the ringing suddenly cut off. An awful stillness spread over the empty room.

He put the receiver to his ear.

And then he heard a voice.

A voice he did not know.

"Ray. Listen to me. Go to the closet and open the door and then come back to the phone. Do it."

Ray stood there, not moving.

"Do it," the voice harshly commanded.

Ray slowly put down the receiver and went to the closet door and hesitated before putting his hand to the knob.

When he did put his hand to it, the knob was icy cold.

He opened the door and then a loud and agonized cry broke out from him.

He shivered violently.

"Alice. Aunt Alice."

She was sitting on the closet floor, looking up at him. A desperate, pleading look on her face.

"Aunt Alice," he said again.

He kneeled down beside her and touched her gently and tenderly, so very tenderly on her pale cheek, and as he did, she fell over backward and away from him, her brown hair brushing against the hanging dresses.

And he saw that she was dead.

After a long, long while he went back to the phone and the voice was still there. He heard it as in a daze.

"Mr. Dawson will be waiting outside the bank at nine thirty tomorrow morning. Waiting for the money."

Ray was silent.

The eyes of the dead woman were before him. Desperately pleading with him. Pleading.

He heard the relentless voice come to him again.

"Speak to nobody. Nobody, do you hear? Now or ever. Or your girl friend, Laurie, will end up the same way as Alice Cobb did."

Ray still couldn't talk.

"Do you hear me?"

Ray slowly nodded.

"Well?"

"I'll be there," Ray whispered.

"Nine thirty."

And then he heard the click.

Chapter

32

Before he left the room, Ray went to the blinds and lifted the slats slightly and peered out.

There, under a bare tree, was a stocky figure.

The figure of Pete Wilson.

The man was standing there, looking directly at the hotel window.

Ray could almost see his dark, melancholy eyes, piercing the darkness.

Ray pulled the slats shut.

When he came out of the hotel, Wilson was gone.

33

He sat by the window in the darkened room, staring out at the night. Hour after hour, not moving, his eyes cold and somber.

Then he heard his mother come softly to the threshold of his room.

He did not turn to her.

"Ray."

He did not answer.

"You must tell me what is wrong."

"Nothing."

"I've spoken to Laurie."

He turned sharply to her.

"You had no right to."

"She said it was nothing. Used the same word."

"Then it is nothing," he said harshly.

"Something has broken the two of you apart."

"Life," he muttered.

She came closer to him.

"Tell me. Please."

"Life and death."

He saw her pale.

"What do you mean?"

"Just what I said."

"Ray."

"Leave me alone, will you?"

"But I . . . I—"

"You what? Life and death broke you and Dad apart. Didn't it happen that way? Didn't it?" he demanded.

She stared bewilderedly at him.

"So why are you coming to me with your stupid questions?" he cried out to her. "Why?"

"Please tell me, Ray."

He rose and faced her.

"Tell you what? That in the end you lose? You always lose, no matter how hard you try in this stinking life of ours. We're all losers. All of us. You lost, didn't you? Didn't you? What kind of life are you living now? You're a loser. Just like me."

He saw the tears start in her eyes.

He turned away from her.

When he spoke again, his voice was soft and agonized.

"Just let me be, Mom. I'm saying things to you I shouldn't be saying. I don't really mean them. Just let me be. Please."

Then he heard her go quietly out of the room.

Chapter

34

He looked down at the medal, a sad, haunted look in his eyes, and then he closed the lid of the box over it. He put the white envelope into his pocket and went out of the vault room.

When he came up to the bank floor, he saw Wilson standing by one of the counters.

Ray went silently over to him.

"You've won, Murderer," he said in a low and bitter voice.

"It's not over yet."

"What do you mean?"

A glint of a smile came into the man's dark eyes.

"Like Yogi Berra says, it's not over till it's over."

"That's a crock," Ray said.

He turned abruptly away from him and walked out of the bank.

Ray paused and looked carefully about him.

The morning was cold and gray.

The sidewalk about him was empty.

Then he saw the dark blue limousine parked across the street and he slowly walked over to it.

This is the end of it all, he said to himself.

The bitter end.

It all started with the skeleton man.

He brought nothing but death and misery.

I wish to God that he had never lived.

Ray saw Dawson sitting motionlessly in the back of the long, sleek car.

The window was down.

"Come in, Ray," Dawson said.

Ray shook his head grimly.

"I have the money. Here it is and goodbye forever."

"Forever is a long time, Ray."

"That's how I mean it to be."

He put his hand into his pocket and drew out the white envelope.

"It's all here," he said in a flat voice. "Every single cent. We're through with each other."

"Are we?"

"Yes."

Then he heard the voice of the driver, a low, harsh voice.

"The man said, come into the car."

"I don't want to," Ray said.

"You'd better."

Ray turned sharply to him and then saw the pale gleam of a gun barrel.

"Do it."

And he recognized the voice as that of the man on the telephone in Alice Cobb's room.

"I'm waiting."

Ray got into the car and sat down next to Dawson.

Dawson reached over and pulled the door shut.

"You can start now," he said to the driver.

"Where are you taking me?" Ray asked.

Dawson patted his knee.

"Just for a pleasant ride along the beach. And a talk."

But the small blue eyes of the man were cold and distant.

Chapter

35

"You were born in this area, weren't you?"

"No."

But I shall die here, Ray thought. You'll see to that, won't you?

And then he drove the thought away from him.

Fiercely.

Fearfully.

They were riding along the beach road now. A pale winter sun had come into the gray sky and the placid sea glittered coldly. The beaches were wide and deserted. Pure and white.

Ray turned wistfully to the road. It stretched ahead of them, empty and alone.

Suddenly a single car swung out from behind and then passed them swiftly and Ray thought he could see the figure of Pete Wilson at the wheel and he thought he saw Dawson nod curtly to the man but the car sped away and soon disappeared from view.

Ray looked out again to the passing beaches and saw no one. Not a soul.

Only a stray black and white gull standing on a sandy hillock and looking out to the sea. It never stirred.

I'm on my way, he thought to himself dismally. To where?

I thought I was at the end of this when I took the money out of the vault box. But there is no end.

Or am I coming to it now?

He heard Dawson's low and quiet voice.

"The money, Ray. I'll take it now."

"What?"

"The envelope."

Ray silently handed over the envelope and watched Dawson take out the crisp bills and count them. One by one.

"It's all there," Dawson said.

"I told you it was all there."

"True. You did. But one must count just the same. Isn't it so, Ray?"

Ray looked away from him and didn't answer.

I've come to hate you, he thought to himself. Hate you and all you stand for. Hate you to the roots of my being.

The car turned off the beach road and then went down a driveway that led to a sprawling wooden building that overlooked the water.

It's the Kent Inn, Ray said to himself. Closed down tight for the winter. I was here with Laurie in August. It seems so long ago. In another life. If I could only see her again.

The car came to a stop in the empty parking lot.

"You can step out now," Dawson said.

"Do it," the driver said.

Ray looked into the harsh face of the man and then at the gun pointed at his head.

He slowly got out of the car and stood there while Dawson unlocked the front door of the building.

They even own the Inn, he thought to himself bitterly. Silently, treacherously, they own everything.

Dawson turned to the driver.

"You stay out here and keep watch."

The driver nodded without a word.

"Come along, Ray," Dawson said.

And Ray felt the barrel of Dawson's gun pressed to his side.

They went down a dim corridor and then crossed the empty and shadowy dance floor of the Inn, past the forlorn bandstand that stood in the gloom, and then into an empty alcove that overlooked the sea.

The pale wintry sun came through the long windows and gleamed onto the bare table and the four chairs around it.

Dawson motioned to one of the chairs.

"Sit down, Ray."

Then he went to the opposite chair and slowly sat down, too.

He took off his hat and set it on the table. Then he placed the gun close to the hat. The gun with the deadly silencer.

Ray thought of the cat with the glittering green eyes.

He shivered. Just as the cat did when it was hit with the bullet.

He fought fiercely to get hold of himself.

Not to let go.

"You're going to kill me, aren't you?" he said.

"Yes."

An icy stillness lay about them.

"Or are you waiting for your executioner?" Ray asked in a low and hard voice.

"My executioner?"

"The one who killed Alice Cobb. And all the other victims you select."

Dawson didn't speak.

A shadowy figure seemed to move into the gloom of the bandstand and then blend backward into the dim corners.

Ray could only see two dark, melancholy eyes.

Only that.

No more.

"You're waiting for Pete Wilson, aren't you? You only kill cats."

"Wilson?" Dawson said curtly. "I don't know any Wilsons."

"Then whatever his name is. Why do you want to kill me? What more do you want?"

Dawson didn't answer him.

Ray's voice rose as he spoke again to the man. "Why? You have the money. It's all there. You said it's all there, didn't you? Why? Tell me why?"

Ray's fist pounded the table and the sound echoed throughout the empty and shadowy room.

Dawson gazed long at him and then a haunted and almost desperate look came into his eyes.

When he spoke, his voice was tight and quivering.

"I'll ask you a question, Ray. Why didn't you hand over the money at the very beginning? Why? You made the death of Alice Cobb inevitable. Just as you're making your own? Why?"

Dawson leaned forward to him, his face tense and white.

"I could let you go free now. But it's out of my hands. It's too late. There are those above me who would make me pay with my own life if I did that. Would you be foolish enough to ask me to give up my life for you? Well?"

Ray was silent.

"You don't answer. Then you see how inevitable this all is. We don't control our destinies, Ray. Life does it for us. And your destiny was to die young. There was nothing you could do about it. Nothing."

He moved his hand forward to pick up the gun

and it was then that Ray heard the shot and saw Dawson flinch backwards and hold his hand in pain.

Blood was streaming down his long fingers.

Ray heard the voice coming to him, as from a haze. "Just stay put, Dawson. Don't move."

And Ray saw the stocky figure come out of the wavering shadows of the bandstand and slowly advance toward them.

"Don't make any mistakes. Your man outside did, and he's dead."

Dawson's face was pale and shaken.

He looked up at Wilson.

"Who are you?" he whispered.

"Treasury Department. I've been following you and your outfit a long, long time. But now I have you where I want you. Every word you spoke is on tape. This place is surrounded. You're through, Dawson."

He turned to Ray. His dark, melancholy eyes softened.

"Come on, Ray," he said gently. "Let's get him out of here."

Chapter

36

"We're human," Wilson said. "And we make mistakes. I made the worst mistake of my career with Alice Cobb. I'll have to live with it."

They were sitting in the back of a quiet restaurant and outside it was getting dark and the lights were coming on in the street.

A lone couple passed by the large gleaming window, huddled close to each other, and then the windy street was empty again.

They all were silent.

Wilson looked at his watch and then motioned to the waitress for the check. He turned back to Ray and Laurie. He sighed low.

"Always. I got to her too late to save her. I miscalculated. I never thought they would kill her."

"Why did they?"

Wilson shook his head.

"She told you she had the evidence. We could come up with no trace of it. None at all. The truth is we'll never know if your uncle jumped or was thrown out of that hotel window."

"Then why did they do it?" Ray asked.

Wilson shrugged his shoulders.

"I'm speculating. After the fact. Maybe it was because she just plain talked too much and it made them uneasy. And when you make them uneasy they eliminate you. Or maybe they thought she had come up with the evidence. We'll never know, Ray. Believe me, they'll never tell you. That's how they are."

He took the bill from the waitress and slowly rose. He seemed to be very tired.

"I've got to be on my way now. Sit awhile and enjoy the place.. As to the money, I have a good hunch that it will end up in your hands, Ray, just as your uncle wanted it to."

He smiled at them and they watched him go up to the cashier. Just before he went out of the restaurant he paused and waved to them. But now there was a sad and almost forlorn look in the man's eyes. And Ray knew that Wilson would never forget Alice Cobb. Never.

Then the man was gone.

Ray sat looking after him a long while.

Laurie reached her hand over to him.

"What are you thinking about?"

He looked at her and smiled and then took her hand into his.

"Nothing," he said softly.

But deep within him, he was thinking of his uncle, and of his father, and of all the skeleton men of this world.

those who died
and those who still live.

About the Author

Jay Bennett, a master of suspense, was the first writer to win in two successive years the Mystery Writers of America's prestigious *Edgar Allan Poe Award* for the Best Juvenile Mystery. He is the author of many suspense novels for young adults, as well as successful adult novels, stage plays and television scripts.